A Grand Design

Other books in the Quilts of Love Series

A GRAND DESIGN

Quilts of Love Series

Amber Stockton

a novel approach to faith

Nashville

A Grand Design

Copyright © 2014 by Amber Stockton

ISBN-13: 978-1-4267-7347-1

Published by Abingdon Press, P.O. Box 801, Nashville, TN 37202
www.abingdonpress.com

Quilts of Love Macro Editor: Teri Wilhelms

Published in association with the MacGregor Literary Agency

All rights reserved.

Library of Congress Cataloging-in-Publication Data has been requested.

Printed in the United States of America

1 2 3 4 5 6 7 8 9 10 / 19 18 17 16 15 14

Dedication

To my best friends, Angie Price Booher and Rachel Margerum. We really don't make sense, but I think that's what makes our friendships work.

Acknowledgments

To my Lord and Savior, Jesus Christ, for bestowing this amazing gift of words upon me. I pray I never take it for granted and always use the gift to bring You glory.

To my husband, Stuart, for sacrificing your time and hobbies to fully care for our little munchkins while "Mommy is writing." Your support of my career is a tremendous blessing.

To Bob Tagatz, resident historian and concierge at Grand Hotel, for the wealth of resources and amazing peek into the Grand's fascinating history.

To Ken Hayward, Executive Vice President, for the packets you mailed and the photos, which helped a great deal.

To my agent, Sandra Bishop, for your unwavering belief and support, even during the time-consuming times of our lives. Thank you for respecting my priorities and still continuing to work on my behalf.

To my family, on both sides, for sharing my books with others and believing in me as an author, even when it means I have to miss family gatherings.

To my editors, Ramona Richards and Katie Johnston, and my critique partners, Joy Melville and Jeanne Leach, for honing my words with your editing prowess and making the story the best it can be. This book wouldn't be what it is without you.

To my marketing manager, Cat Hoort, for giving my words wings and sending them out soaring. I love working with you!

To my fellow writers and authors, and to all my readers, for your encouragement and for rejoicing with me with each new book release. It means more than words can adequately convey.

1

I hate the month of June!"

Alyssa Denham shouldered her way through the revolving door to her office building and onto the concrete sidewalk, her arms laden with bridal shower grab-bag gifts. She should have tossed most of the stuff or found an unsuspecting coworker and bestowed the gifts on her as a random act of kindness. Three office bridal showers in the first three weeks of April. It had to be a record. The predictable wedding invitations arrive in her inbox, and she still didn't have a date for the events. Some of it was her fault. It shouldn't bother her, but it did.

I don't have a date, period.

Every year for the past five years, whenever a wedding occurred for someone she knew, it happened in June. And this year was no different. If June was her least favorite month, then April followed as a close second. As Alyssa stepped out from under the overhang, the light drizzle falling most of the day changed to a steady rain.

"Perfect," she muttered, looking up and down the street for a taxi to the train station. She usually walked, but the gift bags and little wrapped items she carried made the idea impossible. The six blocks would feel more like sixty.

Alyssa straightened as a yellow cab rounded the corner. She stepped forward and tried to free one arm to signal it. When the driver maneuvered toward the curb, relief coursed through her. Just as she reached for the door handle, a Tom Cruise look-alike in a dark gray tailored suit stepped in front of her. He opened the door and held it for a young blonde who could easily pass for a magazine model.

Recognizing the girl as the latest bride-to-be from her office, Alyssa rolled her eyes and sighed. The pretty girls always get the guys—and the cabs. So what if the girl was also in a jam. The young woman and her fiancé might be late for dinner reservations, but Alyssa had an armful of packages—thanks to the two who had just stolen her ride. The cab pulled away from the curb, and the rear wheels sent a spray of water in her direction.

Her favorite cream slacks now sporting a dirty rainwater splatter, Alyssa headed for the corner to catch the city bus. It arrived just as she reached the stop. Balancing her bags on one arm, she managed to withdraw enough loose change from the purse dangling on her arm for the fare, then turned to find a seat. Sandwiched between a woman in a black business suit and stiletto heels with a cell phone pressed to her ear and a fifty-something gentleman with a rounded middle and gray-speckled hair, Alyssa couldn't wait to get home.

If you don't do something besides work and stay at home, you'll never meet Mr. Right. Live a little, Alyssa!

The admonishment from her best friend floated through her mind as she surveyed the other riders. From the shabbily dressed college-age crowd to the handful of silver-haired men headed for retirement, there wasn't a prospect in the bunch—unless she counted the Don Juan type with the slicked-back hair and gold-capped smile who eyed her from across the aisle. At only twenty-nine, she wasn't that desperate yet.

Well, Lord, I would live a little. But on my salary, this is about as social as it gets.

Thankfully, the ride to the train station wasn't long, and Alyssa stepped off the bus. Grateful to be under shelter, she smiled and thanked the man who held the door for her and headed inside to catch her train.

Forty minutes later, she walked through the door to her comfortable two-bedroom apartment. She deposited her armload onto the maple dining room table her grandmother had given her and breathed a sigh of relief. Alyssa flipped through the stack of mail. Nothing but bills and advertisements. She sighed. The usual. Suddenly, a bold word on the front of one envelope caught her attention.

WINNER!

Alyssa stared at the return address. Oh, no! How in the world had this happened? She'd entered the magazine contest on a dare. And now, she'd won? She'd never won anything before in her life. Was this God's answer to her current solitary life, or was He pulling her leg? Alyssa smiled. It had to be a God-thing.

But why this? And why Mackinac Island of all places?

Curious, Alyssa slit the envelope and pulled out the full-color, tri-fold brochure along with a letter. She kicked off her pumps, padded over to her favorite burgundy recliner, and extended the footrest. The one lone accent piece in her otherwise neutral décor. Settled into the cozy comfort of the soft velour, Alyssa scanned the enticing images and well-written descriptions. Just the way the mind of her youth remembered it. As if nothing had changed in all these years. The image of a lighthouse and a few seagulls reminded her of her father and the walks they used to take along the beach. Speculating on the types of people who had walked the beach leaving prints behind had been a favorite pastime for both of them.

Every written description in the brochure promised an unforgettable time. And each picture included a happy couple enjoying the boating activities, horseback riding, rafting, and tennis, not to mention the horse-drawn carriage rides and scrumptious dinner selections. She'd done it all at one point many years ago. Advertising the island as a romantic getaway made sense. But it didn't make her current status any easier to swallow.

Couples, couples, couples! Didn't singles go anywhere anymore? Just once she'd like to see a vacation spot showing someone having a grand old time alone. But as she unfolded the brochure, each new page revealed another toothy twosome, caught up in euphoric delight. And she was a "onesome"—an unsmiling "onesome" at that. Blotting out the images of the couples, she focused on the swimming, boating, and nature walks—things she loved to do and hadn't done since she was a kid. And she hadn't taken her vacation yet this year. Why not throw out the romance and do a getaway for one?

But just the thought of going alone dampened her excitement. She'd played the odd woman out too many times. Not her idea of fun. She stared at the word *two* in the letter as if it were a death sentence. *Two.* Then, a flash of enlightenment tugged at the corners of her mouth. Not a couple. Just two.

Alyssa snapped the recliner into its upright position and reached for the phone on the end table next to the chair. After dialing, she waited for her best friend to pick up. One . . . two . . .

Alyssa straightened as the third ring stopped midway through, and she planted her feet on the carpeted floor. "Libby, you'll never guess what's happened."

"What?" Libby's excitement transcended the distance between them.

"Remember the contest the girls dared me to enter in the latest *Bride* magazine?" Alyssa twirled the phone cord around her fingers and leaned back. "The one promising a chance to win an all-expense-paid trip for two and touted it as a 'honeymoon in heaven'?"

"How could I forget? You almost wouldn't complete the thing," Libby complained. "And I had to dare you to mail it." Her friend's breath hitched. "Wait, don't tell me."

"Yep. I have the notification right here in my hand." Alyssa held the phone away to avoid being deafened by Libby's shriek. "There's only one snag," she said when it was safe. Tucking a strand of her cinnamon-colored hair behind her ear, she pivoted and propped her feet on the edge of the end table. "The getaway is for two."

"Now you listen to me, Alyssa Denham . . ." Libby predictably launched into attack mode. "This is *not* a problem. We'll figure something out. I mean, you are always looking for some excuse to get out of changing your dull routine. If you can find any reason whatsoever not to do something, you will use it. This is just the kind of thing—"

"I want you to come with me," Alyssa interrupted, grinning.

"—you do all the time. And frankly, I'm . . ." Silence filled the line, followed by an incredulous, "What?"

Alyssa smiled. "I said I'm going, and I want you to go with me."

"Alright. Who are you? And what have you done with my best friend? Alyssa would not agree to do something like this so easily."

Alyssa laughed. "It's me, Libby."

"Well, you sure don't sound like the Alyssa I know and love. She would die before she'd make up her mind this quickly. I mean, this is the girl who waited a year before getting her hair cut in the latest style. She got her ears pierced ten years after all her friends did. And she waits until styles go out of season before she decides she likes them enough to buy them. So this can't be Alyssa."

Alyssa crossed her ankles and picked imaginary lint off her cable-knit sweater. "Well, God and I had a little chat about my life on the bus ride home. And when I walked in the door, this letter was waiting. Seemed like a quick answer to me, so I decided to go." Glancing back at the brochure on her lap, Alyssa sighed. "Just maybe, that friend you know is changing. Maybe she's looking for a little excitement in her life."

"Wow. I always said it would take an act of God to get you to break out of the rut you call a life, but who knew He'd take me seriously."

Alyssa shook her head. Leave it to Libby to be sarcastic. They'd been best friends for almost twenty years. Libby's rather boisterous style and brand of wit is what attracted Alyssa. Inwardly, she hoped some of it would rub off on her.

"Come on, Libby. Cut me some slack here. You're the one who's always telling me to live a little. So are you in or out? Answer quickly before I have time to talk myself out of it."

"In," Libby exclaimed. "Just bear with me. I'm still in shock." She paused and took a breath. "And it's free? No catches, no time-share spiels to listen to?"

Alyssa picked up the letter of confirmation, reading it again, barely believing it herself. "It says so right here. And I have the letter to prove it." She reclined the chair back and stared at the stucco finish on the ceiling, the white speckled design resembling the intricate patterns on the sand-washed rocks she had on the shelf in her bathroom. Another reminder of the life she'd lived as a child.

"You seriously want me to come along?"

"Well, who else would I take? I don't exactly have a long line of suitors waiting at my door."

Libby's grin came through the phone line. "No, I mean wouldn't you want to take this trip alone? You never know. Mr. Right could be waiting for you. Speaking of which, where is this place?"

"Mackinac Island in Lake Huron." Alyssa examined the brochure again. "There's even something here about it being named 'Turtle Island' by the local Chippewa Indians who discovered it."

"Turtle Island?" Incredulity laced Libby's words.

Alyssa shrugged. "Hey, I don't write the descriptions." She read further. "Anyway, the brochure says it's a great getaway with lots to do and the perfect place for some excitement." Raising one eyebrow, she pursed her lips. "Somehow, I think the 'excitement' they promise has more to do with their billing this island as a romantic getaway than the kind of adventure you and I could have."

"Do tell."

"There's boating, horseback riding, cycling, parasailing—"

"Parasailing?" Libby latched onto the word. "I can see it now. A skimpy little number with a drop-dead gorgeous instructor standing behind me as I fumble with the sail and play the dimwitted damsel who can't tell which end is up."

Alyssa laughed and shook her head. Her friend's flare for the extreme is what made their friendship work. "And what if the instructor's a woman?"

"Then I'll give her to you while I scout out the *Baywatch* guy."

"Gee, thanks. Some friend you are."

"You know you love me."

"Only the Lord knows why." But Alyssa did know.

Life was an adventure to Libby, and she wanted her best friend to take part in it. Libby usually managed to pull her from her staid and simple existence to create memories far exceeding her wildest imagination.

"So other than the obvious, tell me a little more about this place."

A big ball of fur jumped up into Alyssa's lap. She waited for Kalani to find a comfortable position, then stroked the dark gray Persian's ears, earning a rumbling purr in response. "The brochure says the main hotel was built around the turn of the century, and they don't allow cars on the island."

"No cars? How do you get around?"

"Bicycles, horse-drawn carriages, and your own two legs."

"Sounds like your kind of place. No modern conveniences." Sarcasm dripped from Libby's words. "Wonder if they have indoor plumbing."

Alyssa planted her fist on one hip, startling Kalani. "I appreciate my modernized lifestyle, thank you very much." She gently coaxed the cat to relax. "But, I admit, a part of me would like to get a feel for a bygone era."

"Looks like you'll get your chance." Libby made a sound like snapping her fingers. "Hey, wait a second. Doesn't your grandmother live on the island? And isn't it the same island where you used to spend all your summers as a kid?"

"I was wondering if you'd actually remember."

"As if I could forget. It was all you used to talk about when we first met. I always wished I could go with you just once."

"Well, it looks like you'll get your wish," Alyssa replied, throwing her friend's words back at her.

"Guess so." She paused. "It's been a while for you, hasn't it?" came the soft words.

Libby knew all about what had happened—all except for the real reason Alyssa hadn't returned.

Though her friend couldn't see her, Alyssa nodded. "Nearly fifteen years." Even now, moisture gathered in her eyes. She blinked several times and looked toward the ceiling. No. She wouldn't cry. She wouldn't. She couldn't. It would spoil the elation she should be feeling.

"It's been a long time."

"Yes." Alyssa snatched a tissue from the box next to her and held it to the corners of her eyes. "In some ways, it feels like yesterday. In others, like forever."

"Well, experiences and memories don't just go away. You and your dad had a lot of fun there for many years."

Alyssa sniffed. "And then Dad got sick, and well, somehow the joys of going didn't hold as much enticement anymore."

"Because your mom never cared much for the island. Though I'm not sure why."

"Like you, she preferred the more modern conveniences and easy access to an abundance of stores, outlets, and entertainment options." Alyssa shrugged. "The island just didn't suit her as well as it did Dad and me."

"Probably the lack of cars," Libby intoned. "Still, I think it's been far too long for you, and it's high time you returned. Guess God had the same idea."

Obviously He did. "Well, we've talked about taking a vacation together. And you said you had two weeks coming to you. I can take off as well. It's the perfect opportunity."

"When are we supposed to fly off to our land of adventure?"

Alyssa reached for the letter and scanned the page. "Umm, July seventh." She kicked her feet against the table and swung the chair around, squinting to see the calendar on the wall behind her desk in the corner. "It's a Monday."

Libby rustled some paper. "It gives us a little more than two months to plan. We can have an amazing two weeks, stop in and visit your grandmother, and get into all sorts of trouble. I can't believe this is happening."

"Me, either." Alyssa was almost tempted to pinch herself. She'd wanted a change for a while. This was just the opportunity to help her make it. And it followed all those weddings she'd been invited to attend. After being present to witness three more women she knew being joined in eternal wedded bliss, she'd need a vacation. Winning this trip sealed the deal. "We'll have a blast, whether Prince Charming is there or not."

"You're on, girlfriend," Libby chimed in, obviously infected by Alyssa's enthusiasm. "Mackinac Island, here we come!"

Well, almost. Alyssa had another phone call to make.

⎯⎯∘∞∘⎯⎯

"Oh, Alyssa dear, are you really coming back to our island?"

"Yes, Grandma, I am."

"Praise be to Jesus. My little girl is coming home." Her sniffle was like a knife in Alyssa's gut. "Oh, how I have prayed and prayed for this day to come. I'd almost given up hoping you'd ever return, dear."

"I know, Grandma, and I'm sorry." She shouldn't have stayed away so long. But the days had become weeks, and the weeks had become months, and the months had become years, and before she knew it, fifteen years had passed. "I should have made more of an effort to come see you. What with school and my summer jobs and planning for college, then a career, it's hard to imagine it's been as long as it has."

"Child, there is no need to apologize, though I certainly do forgive you. Your mama needed you after my Richard passed away. It isn't easy losing your soul mate, the love of your life."

Grandma knew it all too well, even if Alyssa could only imagine. First, Grandpa, and then a year later, Dad. And Alyssa had stopped her annual visits, only keeping in touch through cards or the occasional phone call.

"No." Alyssa sighed. "But it wasn't fair to you to be left all alone up there. I mean it wasn't just us. You lost Dad, too."

"Oh, child, I'm never alone on this little island. You should know that. I've lived here all my life and made a lot of friends over the years." The faint sound of *Wheel of Fortune* came through the phone. One of Grandma's favorite TV programs. Hers, too. "Then, there are all the tourists. Some of them provide a great deal of entertainment for me, and I only have to watch or listen to them for ten minutes or so. Now, you stop the line of thought leading you down a path of guilt right this instant, young lady."

Alyssa could almost see Grandma wagging a finger in her direction. She straightened, as if Grandma could see her and would tell her to stop slouching in the next breath. "Yes, ma'am," she replied.

"I am doing just fine, I assure you, my dear." Her voice held all the conviction needed to make Alyssa believe it. "But to tell you the truth, your call and announcement couldn't have come at a better time."

"Oh?" Just how orchestrated was this trip? "What's happening?"

"Tell me again, how long is this little vacation going to be?"

"Two weeks," Alyssa replied. "Why?"

"And dear Libby is going to be joining you?"

"Yes." She sighed. "Grandma, what's all this about?"

"I have a little project for you while you're here."

"A project?" It sounded ominous. Even though Grandma couldn't see her, she narrowed her eyes and scrunched up her brows. "What kind of project?"

"Oh, just a little something to keep you busy in the midst of all the parasailing, horseback riding, and boating I know you just *love* to do."

Yeah, right. Alyssa loved all of the adrenaline-inducing activity most of the tourists sought out as much as she loved the thought of going to three weddings as a solo act. Libby might live for it, but not her. Not in this lifetime. "Now, Grandma, you know me better than that."

"Yes, child, I do. And it's why I know you'll be excited to learn of a little something I've been meaning to do for over a year now, but I simply haven't had the opportunity or the ability."

Why was Grandma being so mysterious? Why not just come right out and say what she wanted Alyssa to do? It's not like she'd have any say in the matter, not where Grandma was concerned. As sweet as she was, Grandma usually managed to persuade everyone to do her bidding and make them think it was their idea in the first place.

"And I suppose Libby and I coming will now give you the opportunity?"

"Yes, dear, it will. You see, I've started a special quilt. One to unite the decades and bring together many different families. But

I can't do it alone. It's going to take you and Libby helping me to make it work."

A quilt? Alyssa swallowed. As in pieces of fabric sewn together in some semblance of a pattern? Her throat constricted. She didn't know anything about quilting. She could barely sew on a button, much less attempt to make something as big as a quilt actually look good.

"Um, Grandma?" She swallowed again. "Are you certain you want me helping with this? I mean, are you sure I won't ruin whatever work you've already begun?"

"Oh, pish-posh, Alyssa dear." She could just see Grandma's hand waving off her concerns. "I know your skill set doesn't exactly involve the fine art of sewing. You leave that part to me." A chuckle. "Though I can't promise I won't attempt to teach you a little while you're here." The background sounds of the TV muted. "No, what I have in mind for you and Libby is to help me collect the various blocks to make up the larger quilt. My old body doesn't get around as easy as it once did, and your strong legs will take you all around the island."

"So, we're going to be collecting quilt blocks from other people?"

"Yes. From each lady who was once part of my quilting circle. I've lost touch with two or three of them, so reaching them might not be so easy. And two have since passed on, but their daughters or sons still live here on the island."

Oh, Libby was going to love this. It had adventure and challenge written all over it. Just the sort of thing to make Libby's day.

"You met most of them when you were a girl," Grandma continued. "So, I'm sure it won't take up much of your time. But it will mean a great deal to me to have your help."

"Of course, Grandma. You can count on Libby and me. We'd be glad to help you."

What sounded like a hand slapping a table came through the phone. "Splendid! I shall begin preparing the list of ladies' names and addresses to the best of my knowledge, and it will be ready when you arrive." She paused. "And Alyssa, dear?"

"Yes, Grandma?"

"I'm pleased to know you're coming for a visit, more so than seeing this project finished. You know I do, don't you, dear?"

"Of course, Grandma." How could she doubt her?

"Very good. We shall be seeing each other soon. Between now and then, you make sure you pack your prettiest clothes and get a fresh haircut. There are quite a few handsome gentlemen on this island, and you never know who you might meet."

Alyssa rolled her eyes. First Libby, and now her grandmother. Was everyone going to try to pair her up? Libby and Grandma were both single, too. Besides, she wasn't taking this vacation to meet men. Not even to meet one man. Now, she just had to convince everyone else of it.

2

The cab driver set their luggage on the edge of the wooden dock and turned to close the trunk. Alyssa added a generous tip to the fare and placed the money in the man's hand.

"Thank you," she said, making eye contact as he pocketed the bills. "I've endured my fair share of cab rides, but yours was the best to date. We appreciate you sharing your wisdom and knowledge of the area's history."

The man raised his hat by the brim and settled it back down over his rather unruly russet waves. He looked a lot like her Uncle Jim.

"My pleasure, miss," he said with a wink.

Same spark of mischief, same distinguished bit of gray from the temples to just above his ears, and same easy-going nature. If Uncle Jim weren't on a photographic assignment in Colorado, she might have to wonder.

"And your name is?" Alyssa asked.

"Frank," he replied. "Frank Reynolds."

"Alyssa Denham." She extended her hand and gave his a brief shake. "It truly was enlightening."

"Well, you two enjoy your stay." He nodded toward the island across the bay behind them. "I believe your next transport is on its way here now."

The driver got into his cab and closed the door, giving them a wave through his rolled-down window as he drove off. Yes. He would get a glowing recommendation from her the first chance she got to sit down and write it.

"Lys, can you believe it? We're actually here!" Libby spun in a circle, her arms outstretched. When she stumbled over her own makeup case, Alyssa laughed.

"Well, we're not there yet. We still have to cross part of the lake." She pointed to where a lone motorboat sped toward them, the white-capped spray behind it diminishing as the boat drew closer to the dock. From what she could see, the name and logo for the Grand Hotel sparkled in pristine, bold colors on the side of the craft. "And it looks like our transportation is just arriving."

Libby shielded her eyes with one hand and looked across the water. "Mmm, and what a welcome wagon it is!" She fluffed her wavy, blonde hair and reached into her designer handbag for her ever-present favorite shade of lipstick, deftly swiping the glossy blend across her lips and stashing the tube in one fluid motion.

Alyssa reached into her own functional purse for her colored lip gloss and did the same. Somehow, Libby gave the mundane action much more flair. After slipping her stick into the designated zippered compartment and clicking closed the faulty snap of her purse, Alyssa brushed her layered hair away from her face and looked up. Two bronzed men in pressed khaki shorts and polo shirts with the hotel and island logos emblazoned on the front disembarked from the motorboat. The lead man immediately made a beeline in Libby's direction. Alyssa sighed as the man offered his arm to Libby and flashed his pearly whites. Typical. Libby always got the attention and the men first.

"Now, this is what I call service with a smile!" Libby glanced back at Alyssa and tossed her a saucy grin, then focused again on her escort.

Alyssa chuckled and shook her head. She should be used to this by now. Being overlooked when she stood in Libby's shadow had pretty much become a way of life. But accepting it didn't make it hurt any less. She bent to pick up her small carry-on and head for the boat.

"Allow me," a low voice said from right beside her.

Alyssa straightened so fast, she lost her balance. Her purse dropped, and several items escaped the confines of the bag. Her left leg flailed and her arms waved, but two strong hands grasped her waist and held her upright.

"Easy there," the baritone soothed.

"Swooning already, Lys?" Libby called out from the boat. "We haven't even gotten to the island yet."

Heat rushed to her cheeks at Libby's teasing assessment of her predicament. She didn't dare look up at her rescuer. Instead, she regained her footing and stepped away. Perfect. The first day of vacation and she was already off to a klutzy start.

Keeping her head ducked and her warm cheeks hidden, Alyssa freed herself from her rescuer's hands and bent down to replace the spilled contents of her purse. Acute awareness of the man beside her made it almost impossible to think clearly. As she stepped onto the dock and walked toward the boat, the man grabbed an armload of luggage and hastened after her. They encountered the other escort who went to retrieve the rest of the luggage.

When they reached the edge of the dock, the man set down the bags he carried and extended his hand to assist Alyssa into the boat. She hesitated and caught Libby's grin as amusement danced across her friend's face. Alyssa swallowed her pride and accepted his assistance. She placed her left hand in the strong grip of her escort and held on to the side of the boat with her right. A tingle shot up her arm at the strength and assurance of his touch.

Careful to maintain her balance, she put one foot onto the block positioned to create steps to the floor of the boat. With both feet firmly planted, Alyssa tried to pull her hand free, but her escort held firm. Captive and with no other alternative, she looked up and met his dark gaze.

With a twinkle in his eye and a charming but lazy smile on his face, he spoke again. "Scott Whitman, at your service."

Alyssa swallowed, unable to respond. This was foolish. She shouldn't be tongue-tied at the first handsome man they met. The playboy where she worked presented a greater risk than this employee. The office Casanova was always stopping by her desk for one reason or another. Libby's nudge from behind brought her back to her senses.

"Alyssa Denham. Pleased to meet you."

The other man stood at the edge of dock. "And I'm the Pied Piper, and your friend here is Little Miss Tuffet." He nodded toward Libby as he shifted his load and waited to stow the luggage on the boat. "Now that the introductions are out of the way, let's get this show on the road!"

Libby laughed out loud, and the awkward moment was broken. Scott released Alyssa's hand. She expelled the breath she'd been holding and found her seat next to her friend.

"Aw, knock it off, Ben." Scott hopped down into the boat with the agility of a mountain lion and reached up for the bags Ben handed down to him. "These ladies don't need to be tortured by your self-proclaimed wit and humor."

"*Au contraire, mon ami*, I believe my sense of humor will only add to our adventure." He flashed a broad smile in Libby's direction. "Don't you agree?"

Libby's expression danced with mischief. "Wholeheartedly."

"And how about our little damsel in distress?" Ben jumped into the boat and shifted his gaze to Alyssa.

Her cheeks warmed again. Maybe she could help erase the first impression of her stumble moments ago. Here goes nothing. She grinned. "It all depends on if your jokes are good or not."

Scott guffawed and thumped Ben on the back. "Busted."

Seemingly unaffected, Ben winked at Alyssa. "Looks like the lady has a quick wit hidden beneath her shy exterior."

Libby looped her arm through Alyssa's and grinned. "Oh, you have no idea!"

Scott took his position by the controls and eased the boat away from the dock. When they cleared the wooden pier, he pushed the lever to the bottom, then winced at the sudden jerk. He should have known better. With a glance over his shoulder, he checked on the other passengers. Ben provided a brace for Libby as the force threw her backward, and Alyssa grabbed hold of the side to keep herself upright. Everyone seemed just fine.

"Sorry," he hollered above the roar of the engine.

"Oh, I don't mind." Libby winked over her shoulder at Ben, who no doubt returned the gesture.

Scott didn't intend to throw any of them off balance. But he had getting to the island on his mind. The faster, the better. Miss Denham's grandmother had nearly talked his ear off that morning on the phone, inundating him with questions about the time the girls were expected to arrive, when he'd be leaving to meet them, and how long it might take for them to get checked in. How was he supposed to know everything? He wasn't their personal attendant or event planner. Transportation was his job. And he did it well.

The misty spray floated in the air around the boat as it sliced its triangle spot through the chilly water. He glanced behind him again. The girls hugged themselves and hunkered low against the seats at the back.

"The water is cold!"

This came from the leggy blonde Ben attempted to shield from the splashes. Scott glanced down at the clipboard hanging near the wheel. Libby Duncan. *That* was the friend's name. Alyssa he knew, but only because of how often Miss Edith mentioned her granddaughter.

"Yeah, it often surprises folks who aren't used to it," Ben replied.

"But, it's July!"

Scott chuckled. Most people had similar thoughts. The warmth of the sun could fool anyone into believing the water would be suitable for swimming. But not up here where the lake was mostly frozen from November to May. And the ice thaw acted like cubes in a drink.

"Don't worry," Scott hollered back at the trio. "The water closer to the island is better. You'll still get to enjoy all those fun activities you were promised."

He couldn't hear a reply, but Ben threw back his head and laughed at whatever Libby said. Alyssa turned away with a wistful expression on her face. The girl had a story to tell. Scott was sure of it. When he'd been told the winner of the romantic getaway prize was bringing her best friend, it made him pause. But when he learned her grandmother lived right here on Mackinac and Alyssa hadn't been to the island since she was little girl? Yep. There had to be a reason.

A warning horn sounded from in front of him. Scott jerked around and braced his foot in time to whip the wheel to the left.

"Whoa, Captain! What's going on?"

"Sorry!"

A few seconds later, Ben's hand landed on his right shoulder, and his friend leaned in close. "You know, it's a lot easier to man a boat when your attention is on where you're going instead of on the pretty little gal staring out at the water."

Scott glanced out the corner of his eye. Ben's smirk said it all.

"You're one to talk," Scott said, pointing his thumb over his left shoulder. "The way you've been doting on Ms. Vogue cover model back there."

Ben thumped him on the back. "Yeah, but I'm not driving a boat toward a dock in a busy harbor."

His friend left, and Scott tightened his jaw. Yep. He'd blown it. Attractive ladies came to the Grand Hotel every summer. These two shouldn't be any different. He'd get them to the hotel where they could check in, and then he'd be back across the lake to get the next set of passengers or off on an excursion, escorting tourists around the island.

Scott pulled back on the gas as they neared the dock and eased the boat alongside the planked platform. Ben hopped out and caught the rope Scott threw him and then wrapped it a few times around the post. Libby approached the step, staring up at Ben as she held on to the bar and extending her other hand up toward him. With an exaggerated bow, Ben took Libby's hand and helped her out of the boat.

"Why thank you, kind sir," she said with a curtsy and a smile worthy of Hollywood.

"My pleasure, fine lady," Ben replied, brushing a kiss across Libby's knuckles.

"All right, Casanova," Scott called up to him. "Why don't you make yourself a bit more useful and help me unload the ladies' luggage to the waiting carriage?"

Not even taking the time for an acknowledgment, Ben pointed toward the two horses hitched to their next mode of transportation. "If you'll make your way there, the driver will assist you into the carriage, and we'll be right behind you with your luggage."

Ben's eyes remained on Libby as she walked away from them. Even as Scott assisted Alyssa from the boat, his own gaze drifted. With the smooth curve of her hips hugged by a pair of white shorts over long and slender tanned legs, who could blame him? Ben cleared his throat, and Scott glanced up. His friend had obviously torn his eyes away first, and he gave an almost imperceptible nod toward Alyssa. Again, her wistful expression had returned, and her gaze was also on her friend.

Scott could have kicked himself. He was such a lout! He scrambled up onto the dock beside Alyssa.

"Miss Denham," he said with hand extended. "Would you do me the honor of allowing me to escort you to the carriage?"

Alyssa looked at him, then at Ben, then at the carriage, and back at him. Her mouth opened and closed. She almost looked like she was going to refuse and tell him she could do it herself, but instead, she nodded, placing her hand in his with the barest hint of a smile. Scott gestured toward the boat and the luggage, and Ben gave him a two-finger salute. No sense in making Alyssa feel even more passed over. He tucked her arm into the crook of his elbow and started them forward.

"Sorry about the bumpy ride back there across the lake. I'm usually a lot better at navigating. Got my mind on other things."

"Oh, it's all right. I didn't mind. I was enjoying the scenery." She chuckled. "I mean, there were a few rough spots, and the careening move you made near the end nearly dumped Libby onto the floor of the boat, but I think the passengers in the other vessel were far more alarmed."

Scott glanced down. Had she seen his inattentive goof? She hadn't been watching him. He was certain. If she had, she would have seen him looking at her instead of at the waterway in front of them. But her bemused grin said otherwise. Should he pursue this train of thought or let it be? She likely wouldn't tell him anyway.

"No doubt," he ended up saying. "But crisis averted, and we still reached the island safe and sound."

"Exactly." She tipped her head toward the carriage. "And I see we have a different driver for the next bit toward the hotel. Guess it means you're off duty."

"For the most part." Again, with the little hints of teasing. This gal definitely had more spunk than she let on. Her flamboyant friend might be overt in her personality, but Alyssa's timely remarks as she weighed in on the situation made for more fun.

After Alyssa took a seat next to Libby, Scott raced back for the remaining two bags Ben had left, and then he joined Ben across from the ladies, settling into the plush gray interior. Ben wrapped on the roof to signal the driver, who gave the reins a little snap, and the foursome clip-clopped their way to the hotel. Scott launched into his tour-guide persona. Time for his well-rehearsed spiel.

"This island has been a favorite vacation spot for over one hundred years. The Victorians made Mackinac Island one of the nation's most favored summer resorts. In the post-Civil War industrial age and before automobiles, vacationers traveled on large lake excursion boats from Buffalo, Cleveland, Chicago, and Detroit to the cooler climates of the island. They danced to Strauss's waltzes, listened to Sousa's stirring marches, dined on whitefish, and strolled along the broad decks of a variety of lodgings."

Libby's eyes met his a few times as he recited the facts, but she often shifted her gaze to Ben when distracted. Alyssa, on the other hand, almost leaned out of the carriage, her eyes wide as she seemed to soak in every part of the ambience for which the island was famous. Although she wasn't the first tourist to react this way, the unabashed appreciation and childlike wonder on her face drew his gaze to her. How long had it been since he'd felt that way about living and working in such a magical place? When had he become complacent? For a few seconds, his memorized script came up blank.

Scott froze.

This hadn't happened to him in nearly two years. Not since . . . no. He wasn't going there. No need to dredge up the past again.

A nudge against his shoulder made Scott turn to his left. Ben stared with both eyebrows raised. "You all right, pal? Snapping turtle snatch your tongue or something?"

Scott shook his head. He had to stay focused. "To accommodate overnight guests, boat and railroad companies built summer hotels, such as the Grand Hotel in the late nineteenth century. And today, it's an experience not to be duplicated. On an island without cars, where horses and bicycles are still the preferred modes of transportation, it's been touted as the slower, more leisurely pace of the past, but with all the amenities of the present. At the Grand Hotel, guests enjoy exceptional service and accommodations, and a full breakfast and five-course dinner are included daily." He looked at both Alyssa and Libby and added, "This is where you ladies will be staying for the next two weeks."

"I'm just grateful to know the hotel has indoor plumbing," Libby said. "When Lys told me about this place, I had my doubts."

Alyssa turned to face her friend. "You knew right from the start about all the amenities." She elbowed Libby in the side. "I showed you the brochure and told you about the themed rooms, the turn-of-the-century decor, and the required dress code for dinner so you'd know what to pack."

Scott nodded. She'd done some research. Good. Or had Alyssa educated her friend from memory? "Yes, the uniqueness of the Grand Hotel and appearing as if time has not affected it is why it almost always sells out, especially during the height of tourist season."

"But there are other cottages and places to visit on the island." Alyssa looked out again at the passing scenery, her attention keen and focused on each cottage, shop, and structure on either side of the carriage.

"Visitors, like travelers everywhere, have come here to shop for souvenirs as well as relax, and Mackinac shops supply them with a wealth of collectible items to take home."

"Like the island fudge?" the ladies asked in unison, their faces beaming as they shared a knowing glance.

"Yeah, but you ladies don't need any of it," Ben retorted. "You're sweet enough."

Libby and Alyssa both rolled their eyes, but Libby also beamed an appreciative smile in Ben's direction. Those two seemed well suited to each other.

"In the 1890s, wealthy Midwestern industrialists who wanted to spend more than a few nights on Mackinac built their own summer cottages on the east and west bluffs." Scott pointed in the general direction of the various homes. "Soon a social life developed, including tennis, hiking, bicycling, examining the local natural wonders, and at the turn of the century, golf on the new Wawashkamo Golf Course."

"What's with all the odd-sounding names?" Libby wanted to know. "When Alyssa read some of the brochure to me, there was also something about this place being called Turtle Island. She told me all about this island when we were younger, but the name never came up."

Ben jumped in before Scott could reply. "Oh, it's because the local Indians at the time saw the island from the Michigan shores as they looked across the straits. This place is full of high cliffs and caves, and from a distance, it looked like a big turtle to them."

"Ooh, caves!" Libby exclaimed. "I can hardly wait to get lost in them." She turned soulful eyes and a pouty lip toward Ben. "As long as you come find me."

"Well, here we are," Scott interrupted before Ben could respond. "The entrance to the Grand Hotel." He extended his hand with a flourish in a sweeping motion. No way could he encompass the vast front porch in the arc his arm made, but they'd get the general idea. Not even a panoramic camera could take in the largest hotel on the island and the impressive grounds dotted with fragrant lilac trees leading to the bluff unless it was an aerial shot. He'd tried. His spliced-together photos in the album somewhere on his bookshelf were the best he could manage.

And right now, Scott wished he *had* his camera. He would've snapped a picture of this moment to keep for all time. The wonder and delight on Alyssa's face was more vibrant than any he could remember in recent tour cycles. Like she was seeing the place for the first time. But her grandmother said she used to be here every summer. Even in fifteen or twenty years, it hadn't changed much. Alyssa's interest in the island obviously had, though. What could have happened to temper her excitement? It might be buried deep, but if the look on her face said anything, the love she held for this place still existed. He might only have two weeks, but he intended to help her remember.

3

All right, we've got afternoon tea on the veranda at three o'clock and a game of croquet on the front lawn with other patrons if we wish to engage."

Alyssa read the scheduled activities from the card the clerk gave them at check-in. She stood next to the white-painted antique oak dresser as Libby made multiple trips from her two suitcases on the bed with wicker-white coverlets to the walk-in closet opposite. The matching dust ruffle waved from the breeze stirred by Libby's movements, and the dark green throw adorning the foot of her bed was completely disheveled. Just watching her friend reminded her of the Tasmanian Devil cartoon.

"We should make sure we have enough time to dress for dinner, too. My grandmother will be joining us."

"You mean she's coming to us?" Libby called from inside the closet.

"Yes. She left a note for me when we checked in saying she didn't want to overwhelm us on our first day."

Another trip from the closet to the bed and back again. "Or else she's just looking for an excuse to dine in the fancy dining room," Libby said over her shoulder with a grin.

Alyssa laughed. "Could be. Although I'm sure Grandma could come here whenever she wished."

"True," came the faint reply. "But not with a granddaughter she hasn't seen in nearly fifteen years." Libby peeked out of the closet with a hanger holding a square-cut, burgundy cocktail dress dangling from her fingertips. "What do you think of this for tonight?"

Muted and somewhat tasteful. "Hmm, it's a bit more conservative than I'm used to seeing you wear." She shot her friend a teasing grin. "But I think it will work quite nicely for this hotel."

"I thought so. I brought others, but for our first night, I figured I'd read the room to see what everyone else is wearing and plan from there." Libby winked, then disappeared again.

Alyssa ran through a mental checklist of the dinner outfits she'd brought with her. Although they hadn't gotten much use, the ones she'd already hung on her side of the closet would no doubt shock Libby. Thankfully, she'd been too preoccupied unpacking her own things to be concerned about Alyssa's wardrobe. Besides, Alyssa would rather explore their uniquely decorated suite than waste more time arranging her clothes.

Like Scott's well-rehearsed speech for the tourists, Alyssa could almost recite the details about the hotel from memory. She reached far back into a corner of her mind. The one she'd locked away years ago to dull the ache. Each one of the nearly four hundred guest rooms had received individual treatment from New York designer Carleton Varney, featuring its own character and style. Varney had been commissioned by the Grand Hotel many years ago and had recently completed a room in the newly expanded wing as a tribute to the movie *Somewhere in Time*, which had been filmed on the island and at the hotel. Richard and Elise. The lead characters in the movie, and the same names as her parents.

Alyssa jotted down a note to inquire about the room the next time they were in the main lobby. If it was anything like this one, it would no doubt take away her breath.

Leaving Libby to continue her back-and-forth trips, Alyssa stepped into the main room and walked from the doorway to the dual French doors opening onto a balcony with an impressive view of the lake. She ran her fingers down the wispy white curtains before grasping the gold handles of the two doors and pushing them open, feeling like a princess about to step into the grand ballroom and greet her subjects.

Alyssa dismissed the fanciful notion and instead turned her attention to the myriad of guests dotting the picturesque landscape below the balcony where she stood. Only a few of the lilac bushes-turned-trees edged the perimeter near the road. The rest grew below the front porch out toward the bluff, but she couldn't see it from her present vantage point. The lush, green lawn was the same, though. And it invited sunbathers and loungers alike. Some concealed themselves beneath colorful umbrellas over wicker tables and chairs, while others preferred the direct heat of the sun on their bare backs, legs, and arms. As she looked to the right, a small group of children enmeshed in a game of tag caught her eye.

Oh, to be so free, without a care in the world except fun and adventure. Alyssa couldn't remember the last time she'd experienced the feeling.

"Hey, how long have you been out here?"

Alyssa turned as Libby stepped through the French doors and joined her. "I don't know. Why?"

"Because I thought you were still in the bedroom, and I was talking to you." Libby planted her hands on her hips in mock indignation. "Imagine my surprise when I came out to find I'd been carrying on a conversation with myself."

Alyssa chuckled at the thought, but sobered. "I'm sorry, Lib. You seemed to be preoccupied with hanging your clothes just right, and I was drawn to the view here."

Libby stepped to the rail and exhaled a whistle. "I can see why." She nodded to the left. "And I thought you were just enjoying the solitude. Never took you for a Peeping Tomasina."

She followed Libby's gaze and saw four shirtless men engaged in what appeared to be a rather competitive game of tennis on the courts below. Heat rushed to her cheeks, even though she hadn't noticed the men until right then, and she took several silent breaths to restore her temperature to normal, hopefully erasing the blush.

"Leave it to you to latch your sights on the men," Alyssa parried in an attempt to hide her desire to steal another peek.

Her friend pivoted and leaned against the railing, then shrugged. "What can I say? I have a radar for men. I can spot them from a hundred yards away with my man-dar."

"You have a radar, all right." Alyssa pushed away from the railing and stepped back into the room. "And sometimes it makes you head in the wrong direction."

Libby joined her, leaving the doors open with the sounds from outside floating up to them on the breeze.

"But it's why I have you. To steer me right and keep me from harm when I go astray." She extended her arms out, hands splayed. "You're the one with the good head on your shoulders. When I follow your lead, I don't get into trouble."

Now how could she not be flattered by such an accolade? Libby had a definite way with words. She managed to turn nearly everything around to flattery. It was impossible to stay miffed at her for long.

Alyssa quirked an eyebrow, but when Libby stuck out her tongue, she laughed. "I'm so glad you're here to share this adventure with me."

Libby raised her arms above her head and twirled in a circle. "And what an adventure it is. Just look at this cushy suite! It's better than any place I've stayed, including the business trips I've taken where I'm staying on the company dime."

"I feel like someone should pinch me," Alyssa agreed. "I've already planned to inquire about seeing some of the themed rooms scattered throughout the hotel." She extended her right arm, palm upward. "But our room alone is more than worth its weight in gold."

"We've got AC, a minibar and fridge, a safe, cable TV, an iron and ironing board, and a coffeemaker, complete with gourmet coffee!"

Libby listed everything Alyssa had already inventoried. But she'd neglected to point out the matching wicker furniture and embroidered throw pillows with scenes of the lake and various points of interest on the island sewn on the fronts, or the framed artwork with ornate frames complimenting the open-air feel of the room. Even the array of flowers on the two tables and the valance surrounding the windows and French doors completed the ambience.

"And you thought you'd be staying in some old-fashioned hotel with only running water and kerosene lamps for electricity," Alyssa chided.

Libby shrugged and offered a conciliatory grin. "What can I say? From the brochure, this place sounded like it might have stuck to the old ways." She whistled low. "But this far exceeds what I thought we'd be enduring for these two weeks."

"So, why are we standing around, gabbing, when we should be seeing everything this grand place has to offer?"

Alyssa led the way toward the door, grabbing her purse on the way. Libby was right behind her. She even managed to lock the door without missing a step.

She snaked an arm around Alyssa's waist and leaned in close. "Let's see if we can find ourselves two handsome hotel employees and guides to help show us around."

And there it was. No matter how distracted she became, Libby always brought her focus around to men. Then again, Alyssa couldn't exactly deny the jump in her heartbeat at the thought of seeing Scott again. Perhaps her friend was rubbing off on her.

———⚭———

Alyssa crossed and uncrossed her ankles and played with the folds of the crisp, white linen napkin on the table in front of her. How much longer would they have to wait?

"Will you stop the fidgeting, please?" Libby grabbed Alyssa's right hand and stopped her from tracing her finger down the edge. "You're even starting to make *me* nervous, and I've never met your grandmother before." She guided Alyssa's hand to the white table-cloth and smiled. "Just relax. I'm sure she's still the same woman you knew when you were a girl. And you've spoken to her more than once each year on the phone. People don't change *that* much."

"Yes, I know." Alyssa sighed and smoothed her hands down the front of her simple, midnight blue dress, then ran her fingers across the circular brooch fastened at the center of the empire waistline. "But I was only fifteen when I last saw her." She cast a sideways glance at Libby, her strapless burgundy ensemble setting off her tanned skin to perfection. "People might not change, but perceptions do. And the woman I knew at fifteen will likely be a completely different woman to me at twenty-nine." Alyssa glanced again at the doorway to the dining room. "What if she doesn't recognize me?"

Libby sighed. "You've sent her pictures, right? And you yourself said she was rather savvy when it came to online communication."

"Well, yes, but—"

"No buts about it. She'll recognize you."

Yes, but would her recognition turn into delight or disappointment once their reunion was complete? A lot had happened in those years in between.

Libby cleared her throat and reached for Alyssa's hand, clasping it tightly in her own. Her friend might have the words to reassure her, but under her nonchalant exterior, she was just as nervous. Alyssa glanced up at the doorway, her gaze coming to rest on the timeless elegance surrounding her grandmother. Clad in a simple pantsuit, with her hair pinned back and up, Grandma could have easily stepped off the cover of one of the many society magazines Alyssa had flipped through back in their room.

Alyssa almost raised a hand to wave and reveal their location, but the maître d' spared her the breach of social etiquette. He nodded at the few words Grandma spoke and extended his elbow to escort her to their table.

"Guess you won't have to worry about whether or not you'll be recognized," Libby spoke low. "Your grandmother is receiving door-to-table service."

The moment Grandma's eyes met hers, a wide smile pushed the fine lines around her mouth toward her cheeks. Slowly, Alyssa stood and waited for Grandma to approach. Moisture formed on Alyssa's palms, and she smoothed away imaginary wrinkles on her gown to rid herself of the dampness. It was bad enough her chest constricted and her heart pounded. She didn't need sweaty hands, too.

As soon as the two stopped in front of Alyssa, Grandma removed her hand from the maître d's elbow and reached out to pull her close. Alyssa's arms went around the older woman's narrow but sturdy shoulders, and she inhaled a unique blend of peppermint and orange. She closed her eyes, letting the scent transport her to the island in her past and her second home for many years. Her home always had a distinct aroma, depending upon Grandma's mood or what emotion she wished to elicit.

"Alyssa, dear, it has been far too long," Grandma whispered.

"Grandma," Alyssa said as she pulled back, the tears gathering in her eyes a mirror of the beloved woman who stood before her. "I wish I'd never stayed away."

Grandma's hands slid down to clasp Alyssa's elbows as a soft smile erased the melancholy of the moment. "Well, the past is the past, and there's no sense reliving it again. Let's put it all behind us now and make the most of these two weeks we have together."

"I like the way your grandma thinks, Alyssa." Libby stood and stepped around Alyssa's chair, then extended a hand toward Grandma. "Mrs. Denham, I'm Libby Duncan."

Grandma's mouth quirked in the corner as she accepted the handshake. "So, I gathered. Alyssa has told me you're not one to beat around the bush." She placed her left hand over their joined ones. "Good for you. My granddaughter can use someone who's not afraid to speak her mind."

Libby winked at Alyssa. "Even if she'd never admit it."

Grandma released Libby's hand and looked to the maître d' who moved to pull out one of the green leather chairs with the broad green and white stripes on the back. "I can tell we're going to get along famously, my dear." She took her seat as another waiter stepped up to the table to assist Libby and Alyssa back into their seats, then cast an expectant glance up at the two men standing sentinel at their table. "Now, Mr. Withers," she began, directing her attention to the maître d'. "Let us hear what is on the menu for tonight."

"Mrs. Denham, it is a pleasure, as always, to have you dining with us this evening." He signaled for a third menu to be placed in front of Grandma, then launched into what was certain to be a mouthwatering presentation of the night's fare. "I'd like to recommend you begin with a chilled Casaba melon and Prosciutto di Parma, then follow with a roasted butternut-ginger bisque. Our classic Caprese Salad is a favorite for many of our diners, and the entrées of choice this evening are the maple barbecue-glazed salmon filet or the spice-rubbed breast of Muscovy duck."

Grandma closed her menu and handed it back to the waiter. "Well, I don't even need to look any further. Mr. Withers, I shall have exactly what you've recommended with the salmon as my dish of choice."

"And for the other two lovely ladies?"

How in the world could they choose from such delectable options? Alyssa glanced up at the headwaiter. "Might we have a few more moments?"

"Of course," Mr. Withers replied. "I shall put in the order for the Casaba melon and bring you a bottle of Sparkling Michigan Wild Berry juice while you peruse the menus."

"Thank you," Grandma replied for all of them. Once the two men had left, Grandma rested her forearms against the table's edge and pressed her fingers into a steeple. "So, tell me. How do you young ladies like your accommodations thus far?"

"They're stunning!" Libby was the first to respond. "From the floral wallpaper to the matching valance over the top of the doors to the patio and the light, airy bedspreads paired with the plush carpet! I feel as if a queen herself couldn't have a finer room."

Alyssa grinned as she glanced over the menu options. All right. Selections made. Now, she could rejoin the conversation. She glanced up at Grandma. "We have been given the Versailles Suite, and Libby's right about the plush carpet. I'm surprised our shoes didn't leave indentations when we walked."

"Oh!" Libby patted Alyssa's arm in rapid succession. "Don't forget about the view."

"Yes, our room has double-French doors leading to a balcony with a beautiful view of the golf course off to the eastern side of the hotel." Alyssa inhaled and exhaled a long breath. "It truly is a sight to behold."

"Well, if you love the suite so much," Grandma replied with a mock pout, "you might not wish to spend any time at my cottage here on the island."

"Grandma, you have nothing to worry about." Alyssa reached across the table and covered Grandma's hand with her own. "Once Libby sees the view from *your* cottage, she'll never want to return to the hotel."

Libby harrumphed. "It better be one amazing view to compete with what we have so far."

"Oh, it will be." Alyssa replied.

Grandma's eyes shined. "And you'll likely be spending a great deal of time with me at the cottage, or at least reporting in each day with your findings."

"Findings? Reporting in?" Libby turned, her eyebrows drawn together and suspicion in her eyes. "Alyssa, dear, did you forget to tell me something?"

"You didn't tell her yet?" Grandma added.

"Tell me what?"

"No, Grandma, I hadn't gotten around to it."

"Hadn't gotten around to what?"

"Well, considering she's going to be your right-hand man, so to speak, you should probably let her in on the plan."

Alyssa shrugged. "I suppose you're right."

"Now there's a plan?" This time, Libby pursed her lips and furrowed her brow as she glared. "Alyssa, you'd better tell me what all of this secrecy is about, or I'll be tempted to find myself another partner in crime for all the adventures I'm going to enjoy while I'm here."

Again, the flamboyance and the drama. Alyssa shook her head. As if Libby would ever leave her stranded while she went off and had all the fun. "Well, if it's adventure you want, Libby, I believe you'll get your wish." She glanced back across the table to Grandma and smiled. "When I phoned Grandma to let her know we'd be coming, she told me about a special project she'd like to complete, and she needs our help."

"What sort of project?" Libby asked.

"Oh, just a little something involving tracking down some rather prestigious residents on the island, spending time in their homes, and rubbing shoulders with a few elite members of what I might call 'island royalty.'" Alyssa slipped Libby a sly glance. "And it means some homes even grander than our suite at the hotel."

Like a fashion diva about to be let loose at a half-off sale, Libby leaned forward to learn more. "Do tell!"

"Grandma?" Alyssa extended her hand across the table, palm up. "It's all yours."

4

Alyssa folded her arms and leaned on the whitewashed wooden railing surrounding the long front porch of the hotel, careful not to disturb the garden boxes of red geraniums. She stared out over the lilac trees and the expansive green lawn toward the shimmering lake water below. The hotel's position high on the bluff *did* offer an impressive feast for the eyes. The lights from the cottages peeked through the trees, and the sliver of the setting sun left an illuminated trail on the water like fireflies dancing on the waves. Alyssa had forgotten about the beauty and the serene atmosphere. How could she have stayed away so long?

Libby slipped her right hand around the same railing and turned to face Alyssa.

"I can't believe you and I spent hours together on a train from Grand Rapids, plus a cab ride from the station in Mackinaw City, and then the entire afternoon," Libby stated, ticking off each passage of time on her fingers. "Not to mention the months leading up to this vacation. And in all that time, you didn't think of telling me we had a secondary purpose to our trip?" Libby raised both eyebrows in Alyssa's direction. "Not even once?"

"To be honest, Lib?" Alyssa angled her head to look at her friend. "I thought I *had* mentioned it to you. We'd talked so much over the past few months, and my grandmother's request had been on my mind a lot." She sighed. "But I guess the speech I'd rehearsed in my head never actually made it to my lips."

"No, it didn't," came the terse reply.

"You aren't angry at me, are you?" Alyssa drew her eyebrows together. "I truly thought you'd love the challenge."

Libby nudged her shoulder against Alyssa's. "No, silly, I'm not mad. Just surprised." One eyebrow rose. "I mean, this is the girl who meticulously plans out every item to pack in her suitcase and is so organized, even her lists have lists."

"You do have a point. And I obviously had a lot on my mind to have overlooked such an important detail."

"Yes." Libby gave her a knowing look. "Like seeing your grandmother after all these years and coming to grips with the haunts from your past that kept you away."

She was putting it mildly. Alyssa had shared a lot with her best friend, but Libby had no idea about the real reason she'd stopped her annual visits. She brushed away a lone tear starting to fall from her eye. The truth had to come out sometime. Just not yet.

"Hey, now." Libby gave her a playful punch on the arm. "No tears on vacation. It's bad karma or something."

"I'm sorry. I guess being here is affecting me more than I thought it would."

Libby draped an arm around Alyssa's shoulders. "Look, Lys. I know there's something you're not telling me. And I know you've got a lot rolling around in your analytical head. I promise I won't press. But when you're ready to talk, I'm here."

As she had been for nearly twenty years. Through the ups and downs of teenage hormone fests, the uncertainties of significant life decisions, and the emotional upheaval of her father's sickness, Libby had stood by her side. She might be flighty, flamboyant, and a little crazy at times, but when it came down to what mattered, Libby was there.

Alyssa touched her head to Libby's. "Thanks, Lib."

"Any time." Libby nudged her again, then pivoted with her back against the railing and her elbows bearing her weight. "Now, enough of all this serious talk. Let's get back to this quilt quest we're going to be embarking on."

Alyssa grinned. Now *there* was the more familiar side of Libby she knew and loved. "You realize, of course, it will interrupt all those glorious plans of skimpy bikinis and playing the clueless damsel to the handsome guides or coaches for the water-related activities." One corner of her mouth jerked. "But I think you'll manage."

A mischievous grin played at Libby's mouth. "Oh, I'll still find a way to scope out the handsome talent here on the island."

"I have no doubt you will."

"And speaking of handsome talent," Libby said with a jerk of her chin in a direction somewhere over Alyssa's left shoulder. "I do believe our escorts from earlier today are approaching." She pulled one corner of her lower lip between her teeth as she focused her attention. "And looking quite dapper, I might say."

Alyssa straightened and glanced down at her dress. She should have changed after dinner into something less formal, or at the least, something more fitting to an evening on the porch.

"Relax, Lys." Libby stayed her nervous fidgeting with a reassuring hand. "You look fine. Not a speck of lint or food stains anywhere to be found."

Alyssa slowly turned and resisted the urge to use the railing as support. Instead, she smoothed her hands down her hips and adjusted her already straight hemline. She raised her eyes just as Scott and Ben came to stand in front of them. Libby wasn't kidding. The two cleaned up quite nicely from the polo shirts and shorts from earlier. And they only wore simple sport coats and shirts with ties over a pair of dark slacks tonight. Imagine how good Scott would look in a midnight-blue suit with a dark wine shirt and contrasting steel-gray tie. Alyssa blinked and shook her head. Now, where had that thought come from?

"Rats," Ben intoned, saving Alyssa from pondering her mental rabbit trail further. "We've been sighted." He winked at Alyssa, but made a beeline again for Libby, stopping in front of her and reaching out to raise her hand to his lips. "But if we have to be caught, I can't think of two more beautiful night-watchers to do the catching. You both are looking quite fetching this evening."

Libby gave him a playful wave of her other hand. "Oh, I bet you say the same thing to all the pretty ladies who come here to visit."

"Touché!" Ben said with a smirk, releasing Libby's hand and not showing any evidence at all of being affected by her rebuff.

"But it doesn't mean we wouldn't still like to hear it," she added with a teasing grin.

Ben's smirk turned into a smile, and he took a small step closer to Libby. She played the game so well. As if she'd read the rule book from cover to cover several times over and had even studied the expansion sets, too. But Alyssa had yet to open the box, let alone choose her playing piece. And would it even matter at this point?

"Speak for yourself," Alyssa muttered.

"What did you say?" Scott leaned toward her and turned his head as if trying to hear her better.

Alyssa's throat constricted. She swallowed, and her eyes widened. Had she just spoken out loud? She looked from Scott to Libby to Ben and back to Libby again. Yep. She had. Great.

"Umm." She swallowed again. What could she say to cover up her goof? "I said we've got two weeks in which to delve," she managed. But it sounded lame, even to her own ears.

Libby jumped into action and moved to wrap her hands around Ben's elbow, sidling close. "Delve into all the fun, she means," she added. "The fun of having two gentlemen such as yourselves to show us around such a beautiful island."

Again with the well-played game, her strategy employed with pinpoint precision. One of these days, Alyssa would have to crack the cover on the rule book and figure it all out.

If Scott wasn't watching her so intently, she might have mouthed a "thank you" to Libby. Her friend caught on to her thoughts and gave an almost imperceptible nod. Scott, on the other hand, continued to silently observe. Alyssa couldn't tell if he'd heard her actual words and was wondering why she'd said them or if he had something else on his mind. With the slight narrowing of his eyes and the downward turn of his mouth, it had to be the former.

But she didn't need his pity or anyone else's. And she certainly didn't need the empty, frivolous words without any real meaning. She'd leave it to Libby with her playful repartee and fun-loving nature. Alyssa much preferred to deal in genuine sentiment.

"So, what brings the two of you onto the porch this evening?"

Libby whistled low. "And what a porch it is!"

"Six hundred and sixty feet from end to end," Scott replied. "The longest porch in the world."

Alright. They could talk about the aesthetics instead. Alyssa glanced to her left and her right. "The red geraniums against the white of the hotel are stunning!"

"Signature flower of the hotel," Ben supplied.

Alyssa glanced between the two men. "Has anyone ever counted them?" If anyone knew the answer, Scott would. He was a fountain of island and hotel trivia.

Ben smirked and splayed his hands in Scott's direction, as if to say, "Take it away."

Scott grinned. "Twenty-five hundred here on the porch, and more spread out about the grounds."

Another low whistle came from Libby. "I don't even want to think about all the potting soil it takes. And the constant watering. I can't even keep one plant alive, much less twenty-five hundred of them!"

Ben chuckled. "Well, let's just say we're grateful to the groundskeepers and gardeners the hotel employs." He pressed a hand to his chest. "I know I wouldn't want to be responsible for the upkeep."

Alyssa nodded. "They do a marvelous job. I remember the view when we first approached this afternoon. Lilacs, honeysuckles, and spireas lining the stair railings, geraniums set against the backdrop of the white hotel, and the expansive porch with the accenting columns. It's breathtaking."

"And it was built in only three months."

"Amazing," Alyssa almost whispered.

Scott looked at her as if she should know all of this. Why would he think that, though? He had no idea about the extent of the time she'd spent on the island growing up.

"You never did answer why you've come to the porch this evening." Alyssa directed her remark at both Scott and Ben, but she left her gaze focused on Scott. Anything to distract him away from his wordless perusal.

As if picking up on her unspoken intent, Scott shrugged and dialed back his focus to look at both her and Libby. "Oh, the usual." His voice held no conviction or emotion. "Performing a perimeter check around the hotel, speaking to guests we've met, and seeing to any personal needs before we call it a night."

"Doesn't it make for a long day of work?" Alyssa tilted her head. "The sun has set already. And you came to transport us from the mainland before noon."

"Is someone keeping tabs on our work schedules?" Ben teased. "I'm flattered you'd care so much."

"No." Alyssa raised one hand and inspected her manicured fingernails. "I'm merely making polite conversation."

"Ouch." Ben pressed his fist to his chest. "And I thought we'd moved beyond such formal talk after sharing a nice boat and carriage ride today."

"It was just part of your job," Alyssa countered. The urge to glance at Scott from the corner of her eye pressed hard against her, but she ignored it.

"Leave it to Alyssa to cut to the chase and state the obvious." Libby extricated herself from Ben and moved to slip an arm around Alyssa's waist. "Don't worry. She'll warm up soon enough, and you'll get to see the charming, vibrant gal I know and love."

This time, Alyssa did look at Scott. Libby's unspoken challenge elicited a reaction from him. As if he was taking it on as a personal goal. If anyone but Libby had said what she'd said, Alyssa would have taken offense. Instead, she angled her elbow up a little and propped it on Libby's shoulder, then leaned in close. "I *am* standing right here, you know."

Libby's head dipped in a succinct nod. "Yep." Her dimple appeared as she pressed her lips into an amused grin and peered over from the corner of her eye. "All the more reason it's so much fun to speak of you as if you weren't."

Alyssa scrunched up her nose at her friend, and Ben guffawed. "You two are quite the pair. No doubt about it."

"Yes, we are," Libby replied. "And it works."

"No arguments there," Ben added, his approving glance meant only for Libby.

Alyssa had no idea how Libby could stand there and accept such an ardent gaze and not lose her composure. If any man looked at Alyssa like so, she'd be addlepated. As it was, Scott's intermittent regard set her on edge.

"So, back to your original question," Scott began, his dispassionate statement effectively dousing water on the lighthearted banter. "We don't always start work first thing in the morning. It all depends on our shifts and what we're assigned to each day."

"Yeah," Ben added. "Some days, we start at the crack of dawn. Others, at sunset. And everything in between. Today, our first assignment on the duty roster was to fetch you two lovely ladies from the mainland as part of the prize-winning package deal you're receiving."

"Oh?" Libby again became the tantalizing tease. "Do you mean the two of you come with the package?"

"Maybe," Ben shot back with a wink. "If you play your cards right."

Oh, brother. She never knew what might come out of Libby's mouth, but where men were concerned, it was almost always flirtatious. Predictable. Just like her own, reliable, eight-hour workday. Nine if she counted her commute. There was comfort in routine. "So, doesn't an erratic schedule ever get exhausting?"

"Sometimes." Scott pushed back his sport coat and slid his hands into his pockets. At least he wasn't taking Libby's bait tonight. One point in his favor. "But we wouldn't do it if we didn't love our jobs."

And it showed. They'd only just met, but from what she'd seen, they gave their all to every aspect of their work. She couldn't say the same about several of her coworkers.

"Scott's right," Ben added. "Some weeks are harder than others, but the perks of the job are more than worth it."

Libby stepped away from Alyssa and did a quick spin in a single circle, the extra yards of fabric in the bottom of her dress flaring out around her, then swaying about her calves. "Getting to work in the middle of all this amazing scenery at one of the most prestigious hotels in this part of the country?" She resumed her stance from when the men had joined them, leaning against the railing as a soft smile graced her lips. "Yes, I'd definitely say the perks are worth any scheduling headaches." Libby shrugged. "Who wouldn't love it here?"

"Well, it does get a bit cold in the winter," Scott pointed out. "And with the frozen lake making water passage impossible, the only people who make it on or off the island do so by helicopter or private plane."

Ben gave a wry chuckle "So, you can imagine the number isn't big at all."

"Sounds restricting."

"Sounds wonderful."

Libby and Alyssa answered together and then shared a grin. All four of them laughed.

Alyssa looked at Scott, who had an amused expression on his face. There was also a certain amount of pleasure, too. As if he'd had her on the scales of interpersonal communication, and something she'd done or said had tipped things in her favor. From the corner of her eye, she caught Ben glancing between the two of them. He was the first to speak again.

"So, Miss Duncan . . ." he began, turning his full attention on Libby.

"Oh, don't you Miss Duncan, me," Libby replied. "I didn't take a two-week vacation and come all this way to be stuck in formal address. Call me Libby." She softened her somewhat sharp words with a smile. "Please."

Ben made a sweeping bow. "As you wish, mademoiselle Libby." He straightened and extended his elbow in her direction. "Would you do me the honor of joining me on a little stroll about the porch?"

She giggled and placed her hand in the crook of his arm. "I'd be delighted."

"But what about your work?" Alyssa spoke up, and the two paused. "Don't you have other guests to attend to or things to wrap up?"

"Nah," Scott answered for them both. "Our shifts ended almost an hour ago." He grinned. "We're off duty."

Well, it would explain the way they'd both lingered there without much concern for any job-related responsibilities.

"It looks like we're good now," Ben stated, again regarding Libby. "Shall we?"

Libby nodded. "We shall." She blew Alyssa a kiss over her shoulder as they left. "Toodles, Lys." She wiggled her fingers. "Have fun."

Alyssa clenched her fists as the pair walked away. Of all the devious, manipulative, and scheming things Libby could have done, this ranked high on the list. The little brat. She was lucky Alyssa loved her so much.

Movement over her shoulder caught her attention, and Alyssa turned to see three children running around in circles with a golden retriever weaving in and out of the trio, barking and wagging its tail. Their carefree laughter floated up on the cool night breeze. In the distance, a mourning dove sang out, its languid, haunting coo filling her with the beauty of the evening. All right. So, being left alone to soak up the calming effects of this island paradise had its perks. Only she wasn't alone.

Alyssa clasped her fingers in front of her. She didn't dare look at Scott, not when Ben and Libby had so obviously left the two of them alone on purpose. The survivalist inside of her plotted possible ways she could excuse herself and end this awkward moment. But no. Let him do the talking. He's the one who got them into this mess with his confession of him and Ben being done for the night. Let him get himself out of this corner he'd backed them into.

Scott took several deep breaths. He should have known. Ben usually pulled stunts like this. But most times, he set his sights on one girl. So, if he went off with her, it suited Scott just fine. When two ladies were involved, though, things got dicey.

Like tonight.

Alyssa clenched and unclenched her fists, then clasped her hands in front of her, visibly relaxing her stiff pose. She hadn't been happy about the turn of events, either. The firm line of her lips, the tight swallow, the narrowed eyes, the clenched jaw. It was almost a nonverbal protest. Then, she glanced over the railing at something she saw below, and her entire demeanor changed.

This softer appearance presented a much better picture. Like some of the artifacts in the Hall of History room inside the hotel calling to him each time he stepped inside. And if she didn't know he stood right there, he could lose all track of time staring at her.

She'd chosen her dress tonight with the same thought process she likely approached most decisions. Practical and simple. No muss, no fuss, as his sister would say. Alyssa probably had no idea just how elegant that dark dress made her look. It hugged her frame in all the right places, the material falling gracefully from the high waist to dance about her feet, clad in a pair of silver shoes with a bunch of crisscrossed straps. And her nicely styled reddish-brown hair fell across her shoulders like one of the cascading waterfalls near the caves and higher bluffs.

A breeze stirred the ends of her hair, and she shivered. Scott snapped to attention.

"You're cold." Scott pivoted on his heel. "Be right back."

He stepped through the nearest doors to the lobby and made his way to one of the supply storerooms, grabbing the first wrap his hand touched. Beating a hasty path back to Alyssa, Scott weaved through a handful of other hotel guests and stopped within inches of where she still stood. He didn't even ask for permission. Just unfurled what turned out to be a shawl and draped it around her shoulders.

"Thank you," she replied, her eyes meeting his for a brief moment before she reached up to grab the edges and pulled the shawl more tightly around her.

And back to the looming silence.

Now what? Scott wasn't good at this kind of thing. He reached up and ran a hand through his hair, certain the strands were standing on end. But he didn't care. They were a visible showcase of his erratic thoughts at the moment. If Ben were here, he'd have some timely remark about the smell of the water on the air or some other nonsense to break the ice and set everyone at ease. But Scott? He did much better when he had a purpose and a focus. This small talk stuff wasn't for him. Then again, maybe it was time to start.

He cleared his throat. "Miss Denham?"

Long, sweeping eyelashes raised as eyes the color of wet sandstone regarded him. "Yes, Mr. Whitman?"

Okay, so she wasn't going to insist he address her by her first name. After all those talks with her grandmother, he knew more about her than she was no doubt aware. But a safe, more formal distance worked for him.

"Would you like to sit in one of the wicker seats over there?" Scott pointed toward a set of presently unoccupied seats.

She hesitated.

"Or, standing here is fine, too," he quickly amended.

"Yes, I would prefer to stand," she said softly.

He gestured toward the space at the railing where she stood. "Uh, may I join you?"

Alyssa glanced down and back up at him. "Of course."

She turned to again face out toward the lake and folded her arms, leaning against them. Scott moved to stand next to her. He gave the sleeves of his jacket a tug before propping his forearms on the edge.

"You know," Scott began. "I'm real sorry about the way Ben stole your friend away. He doesn't always use his head when a pretty girl is around."

Alyssa inhaled and exhaled slowly, her sigh laced with more than just air. Scott turned his head to look at her. This must not be the first time her friend had chosen the attention of a man over her. Yeah, he decided she'd been through this before. And just like his friendship with Ben, she stuck by Libby, no matter what.

"So, how often does she do this to you?"

Alyssa straightened and continued to stare out toward the water. "You mean Libby?"

"Yes." Who else would he have meant?

"To be honest, I've lost count," came the meek reply.

He sighed. "Same here."

Her head and entire body turned to face him. Scott gave her a rueful grin and again ran his fingers through his hair. Oh, to have a low-maintenance cut like Ben, with his military-style spikes. But he'd never been able to muster up the nerve.

"Ben?" Alyssa asked, bringing his attention back to their conversation.

"One in the same," he replied. "In case you hadn't noticed, he has quite a way with the ladies. A skill I have yet to master."

A grin tugged at the corner of her mouth. "So I noticed."

Scott furrowed his brow. Did she mean she'd noticed Ben's gift for charming women or his own lack of talent in that area? Or maybe both?

"Well, as you can imagine, we get a lot of tourists on this island throughout the season, and Ben is usually the first to scout out the eligible ladies." Now it was Scott's turn to stare out over the porch railing. "Most times he sets his sights on one, but sometimes it's two. And that's when I'm left standing with the one he didn't choose. Like tonight."

A soft gasp made him look again at Alyssa. A pinched look appeared on her face. Like someone was trying to remove a splinter from her finger with a pocketknife and not having much success. Wait a sec. What had he just said? He hit the playback on his words. Scott winced. Oh man. He could have kicked himself for the way that had sounded.

"That is . . . I mean . . ." Oh, why couldn't he just spit it out? "Not as if tonight is like all those other nights when I'm stuck with the one Ben left behind." Oh yeah. That sounded *so* much better. And her expression wasn't improving. He should just quit while he wasn't ahead. "Oh, never mind," he said with a haphazard wave of his hand. "I think I should just go." And he spun around in the direction of the stairs leading to the cottages behind the hotel.

"Mr. Whitman?" she called to his back.

Scott placed his hand on the banister and pivoted on his heel. He raised an eyebrow. "Yes?"

"Thank you." She offered a soft smile. "Blundering though it might be, I appreciate the sentiment."

He offered her a mock tip of his hat. "Well, I'll leave you to your peace and quiet. But if you or Miss Duncan should need anything during your stay, please don't hesitate to ask. I'm in charge of transportation, so ask for me should you wish to go anywhere your feet won't take you."

She giggled. "Alright."

"Enjoy the rest of your evening."

"You too," she replied.

Scott took the steps two at a time and landed on the sidewalk at the bottom. At least he'd managed to end on a good note. He glanced back up through the bushes to the partial view he had of Alyssa. And he could take the memory of her sweet face with him until he saw her tomorrow. Even if she didn't know it yet.

5

Now, are you certain you have everything you need?" Grandma perused the items they'd laid out and did what looked like a silent double check against what had to be a mental list.

"Yes, I'm certain." Alyssa placed a hand on her shoulder. "Will you please stop worrying?"

"Map?" Grandma spoke out loud, as if she hadn't heard. "Check. Sample of the quilt? Check. Addresses? Check. Names? Check." She touched a piece of printed paper. "And a master list to cross off names as you go."

"Grandma," Alyssa replied, running her fingers across the polished, but aged surface of the oak dining table. "You've gone over everything at least three times already. If anything, we're likely overprepared." Somewhere, this table bore evidence of her initials she'd once carved in a less visible spot. She'd have to find them when Grandma wasn't watching.

Libby spoke up from across the table. "Well, at least we know where you get your list-making tendencies and your obsessive-compulsive nature."

Alyssa stepped closer to Grandma and draped an arm around her small, but sturdy shoulders, the peppermint from the breath fresheners filling her nose. "And proud of it!"

Grandma turned her head to place a kiss on Alyssa's cheek. "Yes, at least you didn't inherit your father's haphazard organizational style." She chuckled. "I'm not sure I could have handled having you two up here every summer if it had been the case."

"At least we could gang up on Daddy and keep him in line," Alyssa added with a smile. "Instead of us teaming up against you."

"Truer words were never spoken," Grandma replied. She stepped away from Alyssa and moved toward the kitchen. "Now, let me fill some insulated cups with my special lemonade and ice while you girls tidy up and get everything together."

Alyssa collected the items on the table and reached for the embroidered pouch hanging on the back of one of the dining chairs. As she placed everything in the pouch, separating them into the available compartments for easy access. Libby gave a low whistle.

"Phew. Your grandmother is something else."

"What do you mean?" Alyssa asked, remaining focused on her task.

"If I hadn't been here to witness this in person, I might never have believed it." A sound resembling something between a snort and a cough came from Libby. "And I thought you were bad." Her shoes clicked against the hardwood floors as she moved across the room. "I mean, look at this!"

Alyssa looked up.

"Who does this?" Libby pointed at the top of an antique roll-top desk restored to pristine condition. "Who labels pencil holders with 'sharpened' and 'unsharpened' on printed labels? I mean, who has two different holders to keep them separated?"

"It's ingenious if you ask me." Alyssa shrugged. "Saves a lot of time when you need a pencil right away and you don't want to go rooting through your available options until you find a sharpened one."

"So, why not sharpen them all and solve the problem?"

"Oh, don't be silly. Why would you want a bunch of sharpened pencils you're not using, when you can only use one at a time?"

Libby rolled her eyes and gave a dismissal wave. "I give up. You two are like two peas in a pod. And both of you are hopeless."

"Lib, my grandmother might seem eccentric, but she didn't have much of a choice." Alyssa moved around the table to lean against the other side. "She wasn't much more than ten when the war in Europe broke out, and her youngest brother had just been born with a bad case of what she called intestinal indigestion."

Libby scrunched up her nose and grimaced, propping her right arm on top of the desk. "Sounds awful."

"From what she told me, it was. As a baby, he couldn't keep much down, and because of rationing, he wasn't getting the nutrients he needed, so his immune system was low. It meant he got sick a lot, so their mother insisted on their home being completely free of germs."

"As if it's possible to do so."

"Exactly," Alyssa replied. "But you couldn't tell her so." She shook her head. "Several different prescriptions of medicine from their doctor helped keep some of the symptoms at bay. And each one had different dosages at different times." Alyssa had heard this story several times growing up when she'd questioned Grandma about the very same things. "For years, until her brother grew strong enough to start fighting off the infections on his own, and his body had healed from the intestinal issues, Grandma scrubbed, dusted, disinfected, mopped, washed, and kept things organized. She was the oldest, so a lot of the responsibilities fell to her, especially with their father serving in the war and their mother having to work to help pay for all the medications and doctor's visits."

"Wow, I had no idea."

"I didn't either when I spent my first summer here." Alyssa crossed her arms. "But once she explained everything, it all made sense."

"Yeah?" She pursed her lips and stuck her tongue against her cheek. "So, what's your excuse?"

Alyssa stuck out her tongue. "I should've expected that."

Libby threw back her head and laughed. "You walked right into it. I have absolutely no sympathy." She shoved away from the desk and crossed the room to push the lace curtains aside and look out one of the front windows. "You weren't kidding about the view."

Oh good. A change of topic. Alyssa didn't relish the thought of taking another walk down memory lane this morning. Grandma's place alone stirred up enough. With the furniture set in the same layout as when she'd been there as a child, and the pictures of Daddy and the rest of the family all over the place, melancholy came knocking at her mind's door. She brushed it aside and joined Libby at the window, mirroring her friend's stance.

"Didn't I tell you?"

Alyssa smiled at the myriad of flower beds and neatly shaped bushes arranged in a curving pattern around the perimeter. Two hand-carved stone benches sat on opposite sides of the yard, enmeshed in the floral cornucopia. She'd spent many an afternoon on those benches, reading the latest Nancy Drew book or daydreaming. And the single tree Daddy had planted had grown to nearly thirty feet, now sporting a circular array of colorful flowers at its base as it stood sentinel over the landscape. Lush, green grass covered the remainder and flowed to the front walk where the edge had been trimmed to perfection.

"Just the way I remember it."

Libby angled her head. "I can see now why you loved coming up here so much."

Alyssa sighed. "Yeah. It *is* beautiful."

"And I will say one thing. In spite of your grandmother's odd-ball idiosyncrasies, she knows how to pick the spots, and she's got a fantastic eye for gardening."

"Why, thank you, Libby," Grandma said as she rejoined them in the main room. She set two large, stainless steel cups on the table next to the pouch. "Here are your lemonades."

Both girls turned at the same time and again faced the interior of the home.

"You know," Grandma continued. "I can't take credit for everything around the outside of the house." She nodded at Alyssa. "Alyssa here supplied her own input and suggestions when it came to making this place our own."

Libby's eyebrows rose. "Ah, another one of your hidden talents, Lys?"

Alyssa gave her friend a wry grin. "Not exactly. I had the help of gardening books and magazines, and of course, the other cottages here on the island for inspiration. Unfortunately, HGTV wasn't around then, or I would have used it, too."

"Well, this place could easily qualify for a magazine spread." Libby glanced again out the window. "No doubt about it."

"She and her father were up here so often, I wanted them to feel every bit at home as they did in their house on the mainland."

Alyssa moved to her grandmother's side and gave her a sideways hug. "And you succeeded, Grandma. So much so, when the end of summer came, I didn't want to leave."

Grandma brushed back several strands of Alyssa's hair and laid a hand aside her cheek. "Nor did I want you to go, my dear. You reminded me so much of the daughter I lost, and it was wonderful to capture that time with you each year." She sighed. "The saddest moments I can recall were those late-August good-byes, standing on the dock and watching the boat whisk you across the lake to the mainland, taking you away from me for the next nine and a half months."

Alyssa leaned against her grandmother's age-roughened hand. "If I could have stayed, Grandma, I would have."

Grandma smiled. "I know, child. But school and life with your family called, and you had to go back." Her smile dimmed, and moisture gathered at the corners of her eyes. "Then the year came when you didn't return, and I had to change my expectations for those summer months and establish a new routine."

Alyssa rested her head on her grandmother's shoulder. All that hurt and pain for no reason other than Alyssa couldn't bring herself to return to so many memories without her father there beside her. She hadn't known until today just how selfish she'd been. Grandma had faced those memories, too, only thanks to Alyssa she'd done it alone.

"Oh, Grandma, I am sorry," she whispered.

"Nonsense," Grandma squared her shoulders and reached for a handkerchief to wipe the tears from her eyes. "What's done is done, and as I said at dinner last night, it's all in the past. What's important is you're here now, and we can make up for lost time."

A knock sounded at the front door.

Libby looked out the window and squealed. "Ooh, Lys, it's a private horse-drawn carriage!" She peered in several directions and even pressed her nose against the glass. "But I don't see the driver anywhere."

Grandma smiled. "It's your transportation for the day. And Libby, the driver is the one who knocked."

Libby offered a sheepish grin. "Oh, right." She clapped her hands and did little jump. "I can hardly wait."

"Our transportation?" Alyssa drew her eyebrows close. "But I figured we would just walk."

"Alyssa, dear, this island might not be large compared to some of the cities you've no doubt visited, or even the city where you work, but the elevation changes drastically in places." She folded her handkerchief with meticulous precision. "Besides, you two are on vacation. You shouldn't have to endure a workout while you're doing your old Grandma a favor." She nodded, "Now, be a dear and answer the door, please?"

"Yes, ma'am." Alyssa stepped around the table and walked to the front door. She turned the knob and swung it open, and her breath hitched at the man who stood on the other side of the screen. "Mr. Whitman?" she croaked.

"Good morning, Miss Denham," he replied with an easy smile.

"Wait a minute." Libby rushed from the window to the door and stood beside Alyssa. "Scott's here?" She bobbed her head like one of those dolls in the back windows of cars. "Does this mean Ben's here, too?"

"No, Libby, it's just me today." He returned his gaze to Alyssa. "And please, call me Scott. I meant to say something last night, but well . . ." He dipped his head a little and gave her a rueful grin. "You know how that went."

She giggled. "Okay. And you can call me Alyssa." She felt, rather than saw, Libby's stare. There'd definitely be questions later. But right now, she had a few of her own. She peered over Scott's shoulder at the carriage with an unfamiliar logo emblazoned on the side waiting at the end of the sidewalk. "This isn't a hotel carriage." Her gaze returned to him and the pair of pressed slacks he wore topped by a short-sleeve lightweight pullover with three buttons left undone at the neck. "And you're not in uniform. So, what brings you here?"

"I'm not working for the hotel this morning," he replied. "I'm wearing my other hat, so to speak."

"Other hat?"

"Yes, as a private coach for hire. Your grandmother is one of my regulars." He did a little bow. "Arch Rock Carriage at your service."

"Alyssa," Grandma called from behind her. "Are you going to make Scott wait on the stoop while you grill him with twenty questions, or are you going to invite him inside?"

She winced at the admonition and reached for the latch to the screen door. "I'm sorry, Mr. Whit . . . I mean, Scott." Alyssa pushed it out, and he grabbed hold to open it the rest of the way. "Please, come in."

"Thank you," he said with a nod.

Alyssa couldn't help but watch him as he stepped past her and Libby and made a beeline for her grandmother. Back straight, head held high, confident swagger. Quite a change from the bumbling uncertainty of last night and even from the way he'd greeted her just now. He and her grandmother had more of a relationship than she'd suspected.

"Miss Edith," Scott said as he placed a kiss on Grandma's cheek. "I smell fresh-squeezed lemons." He grinned. "Does it mean you've been making your delicious lemonade again?"

Grandma twittered under Scott's amiable attention. "As a matter of fact, yes." She reached around the wall and retrieved a third cup identical to the two sitting on the table. "And I've poured a fresh glass for you as well as two for the girls." She nodded toward the floor. "There's also a full Mason jar in there."

Scott reached down at his feet and lifted a wicker picnic basket. "I take it this is going with us today?"

Now where had the basket come from? Alyssa glanced from the floor to her grandmother and back to the floor again as Scott grabbed hold of the handle and lifted the basket. And how had she not seen it?

"Yes," Grandma replied. "I wasn't certain how long you'd be gone, and I didn't want you three to get hungry."

"Thank you." Scott gave the basket an appreciative sniff. "I'm certain whatever you packed will be delicious, and it's sure to come in handy." He tucked his cup under his arm then grabbed and secured the other two cups. "I'll get these things stowed, and then we can be on our way." Three long strides brought him to Alyssa and Libby again. "Excuse me, ladies," he said as he shouldered his way through the doorway and outside once more.

Definite difference all around. He was relaxed and completely at ease around Grandma. Confident even. And a coach for hire? Did it mean Grandma had somehow managed to make certain he was the one to greet her and Libby at the dock yesterday? She wouldn't put it past her. But this side of Scott. Alyssa couldn't decide which one she liked more—the charming and bumbling hotel employee or the self-assured and assertive entrepreneur who'd surprised her with his arrival this morning.

"Alyssa, dear, close your mouth. And you, too, Libby. You're both going to catch flies."

"Wow," was all Libby could say as she continued to stare down the walk after Scott.

Grandma's amused chastisement and Libby's verbal response reminded Alyssa she wasn't the only one in the room at the moment. She had to pull herself together. With a deep and cleansing breath, the fresh intake of oxygen helped clear her head. She walked to the table and grabbed the strap of the pouch with all their papers tucked safely inside. After slipping the strap over her head and tucking the pouch against her hip, Alyssa looked at her grandmother.

"Have a pleasant morning, my dear," Grandma said with a twitch of her lips and a mischievous gleam in her eyes.

Yep. Grandma was definitely behind all of this. But Alyssa refused to be baited. Stick to the facts. They were safe enough. "As long as the weather cooperates, I'm sure we will," Alyssa replied. "And we'll call if we have any problems." She kissed Grandma's cheek. "By the time we return, we should have two new blocks for your quilt."

"Splendid."

"Now, I believe our carriage awaits." Alyssa spun and headed back for the door, snagging Libby around the waist as she reached for the latch. "Come on, Libby. We've got work to do."

"Good-bye, Mrs. Denham," Libby called over her shoulder as the two made their way down the sidewalk.

As soon as they came within ten feet of the carriage, Scott hopped down from his perch with the grace of a cougar and swung open the door. He lowered the step block and extended his hand to assist them both into the carriage, bestowing a grin upon Alyssa as he delivered her inside. Once she and Libby were settled, he secured the block, latched the door, and resumed his perch. Taking the reins in hand, he glanced down at them over his shoulder.

"I take it you have the first destination already selected?"

Alyssa just stared. A second later, sharp pain shot up her leg from her shin. "Ow!" She reached down to rub the injured leg and glared at Libby. "What was the kick for?"

"Scott asked you a question, and you were just daydreaming."

Alyssa shook her head. No wonder he'd been looking down at her as if expecting an answer. Now, what was it he'd asked? Oh, right. The address. "I'm sorry," she muttered as she reached into the pouch and pulled out the master list. "Yes, we're going to Maple Ridge Street."

"Maple Ridge Street," Scott echoed and turned to face forward. "It's over near the airport. Got it." With a flick of the reins, they were off.

As they made their way down Huron Road, Alyssa stared off to the left and down at the main part of town at the water's edge. If Scott took the route she remembered, he'd stay on these bluffs above Main Street and wind around behind the Grand to Annex Road.

Libby wasted no time at all sinking into the cushiony softness of the leather seats. "Mmm." She linked her fingers behind her head and stretched out her long legs, staring up at the blue sky above. "This day keeps getting better and better."

"The jury's still out on my assessment," Alyssa replied. She allowed the soft leather to support the weight of her back as she leaned her head against the pillow rest.

"Aw, come on, Lys." Libby turned her head, but left it lying against the top of the seat. "You have to admit, this side of Scott is much more appealing." She grinned. "And those little grins he gave you are saying something, too."

"Keep your voice down," Alyssa spoke through gritted teeth. "I don't want him to know we're talking about him."

Libby chuckled. "As if he doesn't already know."

"Well, we don't need to make it obvious."

Her friend rolled her eyes. "All right. I'll wait until he's out of earshot before you and I have ourselves a little chat." She sighed. "For now, I'm just going to enjoy the ride."

It sounded like a good idea. A nice, quiet, peaceful drive. Alyssa closed her eyes and let the clip-clop of the horse's hooves soothe her. The roar of a private jet echoed in the sky above, and the warm breeze washed over them, carrying with it the misty moisture of the lake. Alyssa inhaled the fresh scent and attuned her ear to the distant sound of waves lapping at the island's shoreline. So different from the salty sea air along the coasts. The hum of motorboats bouncing on the water blended with the snapping of flags flying from homes and buildings nearby, and the *ching* of a pull cord slapping against a flagpole reminded Alyssa of the bell on the bike she rode around the island as a girl.

Other carriages passed as they wove their way to the west side of the island. Bicycle wheels whirred with the rubber against the pavement, and the occasional single-occupant cart came whizzing past. Every few hundred feet or so, children's giggles or the excited bark of a dog floated on the air to them. Such a simple and carefree way of life.

"We're here," Scott announced and brought the carriage to a stop. He set the brake and vaulted from the seat.

Libby sat up and looked around. "Well, this was fast."

As Scott helped Libby down first, Alyssa gazed over their heads to the simple but elegant cottage in front of them. She fixed her eyes on the lone figure between them and the cottage as Scott reached back up to assist her from the carriage. A woman wearing a wide-brimmed hat and gardening apron stood in the front yard spraying water from a hose on several areas of her flower garden. When Scott reached over the white picket gate to unlock the latch, the woman looked up. She shielded her eyes and squinted, peering at each one of them in turn. Then her gaze landed on Alyssa, and a broad smile spread across her face. She dropped the hose and crossed the distance to meet them.

Dottie Janson. The first name on Grandma's list. A little older and a bit more gray hair, but still the jovial and warm motherly type Alyssa remembered.

Dottie brushed her hands on her capri pants then reached out and took Alyssa's hands in her own. "Well, if it isn't little Alyssa Denham, all grown up and back on the island to come say hello." She tilted her head and gave Alyssa a once-over. "You look just like your grandma when she was your age."

"Good morning, Mrs. Janson," Alyssa replied.

"Oh, don't you Mrs. Janson, me, Alyssa." She waggled a finger in her direction. "Miss Dottie was good enough for you when you were a little girl, and it's good enough for you now."

Laughter bubbled up and escaped through her lips. "Miss Dottie, this is my best friend, Libby Duncan." She turned to include Scott. "And Scott Whitman is the one who brought us here."

"Pleased to meet you, Miss Duncan." Miss Dottie shook hands with both Libby and Scott in turn. "And Mr. Whitman. Of Arch Rock Carriage Services, if I remember correctly?"

Scott nodded. "Yes, ma'am."

"Your reputation precedes you, young man." A look of silent approval passed between them. "Several people have recommended you more than once." She winked. "I might just have to see what all the fuss is about."

He reached into his shirt pocket and withdrew a business card. "Please do," he said as he handed Miss Dottie the card. "My office is located one block north of Main on McGulpin Street, just down from the Butterfly House."

Dottie slipped the card into the pouch of her apron and angled toward her house. "Come, come. Let's go inside. I'll pour us some tea while you catch me up on what's happened since I saw you last and tell me all about the reason for your visit."

6

Miss Dottie scooted forward on her whitewashed bistro chair and reached for the silver tea service on the closer of two round tables. As she served each of her guests, Alyssa looked around the covered patio. The lattice work in a filigree pattern wove its way up each of the three trellises to the vinyl roof. Artfully arranged clinging vines meandered through the pattern and hugged tight to the rooftop, their potential for overtaking the patio kept under control with careful trimming.

"Alyssa?" Miss Dottie spoke, and Alyssa turned her attention to their hostess. "Iced tea for you as well?"

"Yes, thank you," she replied as she accepted the tall glass with condensation already forming on the outside. She didn't know if she should wait until Miss Dottie again asked for the particulars of their visit, or if she should go ahead and begin on her own.

"Now, please, Alyssa. Since we've already done our catching up while waiting for the tea to steep, tell me what project your grandmother has started now and what part you're playing in it." Miss Dottie smiled. "For I know it couldn't be anything but Edith's doing to bring you out here on what is likely a vacation visit."

Miss Dottie had saved Alyssa the trouble of broaching the topic herself.

Libby laughed. "She knows your grandmother well, Lys."

"I'd better," Miss Dottie replied. "We went to the same grade school, lost touch in high school when my family sent me to St. Ignace for those four years, then reunited at the university where our shared love of quilting led to the creation of the quilting bee we formed while attending there."

Miss Dottie couldn't have provided a better segue even if she'd already been told about the details of the project. Alyssa took a sip of her tea then set the glass in the palm of her hand. "The bee is exactly why we're here, Miss Dottie."

"Oh? But we haven't met together in what . . ." She tapped a wrinkled finger to her lips. "It's been sixteen years, I believe." She leaned forward. "Do tell."

Alyssa had no idea how much Miss Dottie already knew. Grandma hadn't exactly had the time to brief her on every member of the group or the specifics of what had caused them to disband. "When I phoned Grandma to tell her Libby and I were coming for a visit—"

"She'd won a bridal contest from a magazine," Libby added, jutting her chin in the air an inch or two. "I dared her to enter it."

Miss Dottie's eyebrows rose. "A bridal contest?" Her gaze immediately shifted to Scott, then to Alyssa, then back to Scott again.

Heat warmed Alyssa's neck at the unspoken question. Great. Just what she didn't need. People thinking she and Scott were a couple. Bad enough Scott had known about the contest even before they'd arrived. But did Libby have to bring it up again? Alyssa opened her mouth to correct the misconception, but movement to her right made her close it.

Scott raised his hands in mock surrender, one of them still holding his glass. "Don't look at me. I live here on the island, remember?"

"No, Miss Dottie, it's not what you think," Alyssa added. "I'm not getting married. I'm not even engaged. Libby here," she said, with a glare in her friend's direction, "thought my life needed a little excitement." She shrugged. "I don't usually turn down a dare, so I entered. I never believed I'd win. And when I found out, I dragged Libby along with me."

"Ah, and now you're both here." Miss Dottie leaned back in the chair, leaving her free hand resting on the table's edge. "Soaking up the sun, relaxing in the middle of summer, enjoying some time off from your no-doubt hectic lives back home, and Edith has you out doing her work for her."

"Not exactly." Alyssa took another sip of tea and returned the glass to her palm. The cool freshness moistened her mouth and lips. "Grandma told me the members of the bee had once talked of putting together a quilt with everyone contributing a block or two to represent either the special friendship you shared or something unique about the group itself."

Miss Dottie narrowed her eyes, then nodded. "Ah yes. A friendship quilt. I do remember discussing it not long before we all parted ways."

"Well, Grandma said it's been on her mind for a while now, and she's asked Libby and me to be her legs by visiting each of the women who were part of the original group and collecting the squares." Alyssa splayed her left hand in a loose wave. "How could I refuse?"

"With Edith?" Miss Dottie chuckled. "You couldn't. She wouldn't let you."

Alyssa and Libby both laughed and answered at the same time. "Exactly!"

"And where you do come into all of this?" Miss Dottie directed her question at Scott, who'd only said a few words since they arrived.

"Oh, I'm just the driver," he answered. "Miss Edith hired me."

"Mmm," was all Miss Dottie said. A few seconds later, she snapped her fingers. "You know, I did make a square a while back, but for the life of me, I haven't the faintest idea where it is right now." She glanced at the sliding glass door leading into her home. "How long are you ladies staying on the island?"

"Two weeks," Alyssa replied.

"Do you think perhaps you could return in three or four days? I'm certain I'll have found the square by then. If not," she said with a shrug, "I'll simply whip out another one to be used."

Libby made a nasal sound resembling something between a sniff and a snort. "You say it like it's such an easy thing to do."

"But it is," Miss Dottie replied, looking back and forth between the two girls. "Don't either of you sew?"

"They didn't teach that course in business school," Alyssa answered.

"Well, if I know Edith . . . and I do." Miss Dottie smiled. "She'll have you working the basics of needle and thread before your visit ends." She reached for the pitcher, but Scott beat her to it and refilled her glass. "Thank you, Mr. Whitman."

"My pleasure," he replied, then turned to Alyssa and Libby. "Do either of you want more?"

Libby held up her glass. "Yes, I would."

Alyssa shook her head. "None for me. Thanks."

Despite standing not eighteen inches away from her, Scott averted his gaze. She tried to catch his attention by dipping her head to look up at him, but he didn't take the bait. Sitting here sipping tea wasn't exactly a preferable morning activity for a guy like him, but he could have waited with his carriage. Why had he chosen to accompany them instead?

Miss Dottie took another sip of tea and wet her lips. "You know, Edith was the heart and soul of our group. When anything happened to any one of us, she was there, rallying the rest of the group to bring us meals, come to the hospital during visiting hours, deliver flowers, or pay a visit to each other's homes."

Libby released a soft sigh. "Sounds like a pretty special group of ladies."

Moisture gathered in Miss Dottie's eyes. "It was. Nothing could break us up." Her breath hitched as she looked at Alyssa, a frown turning down the corners of her mouth. "Until your grandpa got sick." Her fingers tapped the glass she held. "She'd been the one to hold us all together, but with her attention fully focused on Henry, Maureen Corbitt decided it was time for a new leader." Her lip curled. "And she gladly stepped into the role." She sighed. "Several other ladies agreed, but most of us didn't, and it caused a great deal of disagreement. I've always wondered if we hadn't let ourselves go down the path we did if we would still be together today."

Alyssa's lips parted at Miss Dottie's confession. Grandma had never mentioned any of this. The way Grandma had put it, it sounded as if time and life had intervened, not an intentional division among the group members.

"This Maureen sounds like a real peach of a woman," Libby muttered.

"Right when Edith needed us the most," Miss Dottie continued. "We let her down."

Alyssa reached across and patted the weathered hand. "Please don't blame yourself, Miss Dottie. I'm sure Grandma holds no hard feelings. If she did, do you think she'd be trying to recapture the memories in this special quilt?"

Miss Dottie nodded. "You're absolutely right." She sniffed. "And I'm sorry. You come here on a joyous errand, and I manage to drag down the mood with all my melancholy thoughts."

Alyssa held up one hand. "No need to apologize on our accounts, Miss Dottie." She glanced at Libby, then Scott, who both nodded, before returning her gaze to their hostess. "We can all understand. There must be at least a half dozen 'if only' or 'what ifs' you could ask yourself, and not a single one of them would bring you any greater comfort." She paused, waiting for Miss Dottie to raise her chin. "As Grandma would say, 'The past is the past. Let's focus on the here and now.'"

A slow smile spread across Miss Dottie's face. "It sounds exactly like Edith, my dear." She slapped her thigh. "And you are absolutely right." She stood, and the rest of them followed suit. "Now, I don't wish to be rude, but I have a hair appointment in about thirty minutes, and I need to freshen up first."

No one spoke for several moments as they each drained their glasses and set them on the service tray. Miss Dottie lifted the tray and looked at each one of them in turn.

"Please, do come back in a few days, and I'll have the quilt block for you." She turned to go inside, then pivoted to face them again, nodding to the south side of the cottage. "If you don't mind letting yourselves out, you'll find a gate there to lead you around to the front of the house. Follow the stepping-stones. They'll take you right to your carriage."

"Thank you, Miss Dottie," Alyssa replied. "It's been nice visiting with you."

"Yes, thank you for the tea," Libby added.

"You are most welcome, dears." She looked at Libby. "Again, Miss Duncan, it was a pleasure meeting you." Moving on to Scott, she added, "And you, young man. I'm sure you'll be hearing from me soon."

Scott touched one finger to his forehead, as if tipping an imaginary hat, before walking ahead and holding open the gate.

"Mouthwatering lunch, here we come!" Libby announced as she stepped in front of Scott.

"Thank you." Alyssa nodded at him and trailed in Libby's wake. "So, what makes you think our lunch will be mouthwatering?"

Libby glanced over her shoulder but continued to prance toward the carriage. "Because I could smell it all the way over here." She grinned. "I can hardly wait to see what your grandmother packed."

"And I know the perfect place," Scott chimed in as he caught up with them.

———

Scott plopped down on the grass a few feet away from Alyssa, and she jumped.

"Sorry. I didn't mean to scare you."

She waved him off. "It's all right. I must have been daydreaming."

He held his lemonade cup in one hand and the picnic basket in the other as he assessed the secluded spot. They'd driven past where a lot of other tourists or island residents had chosen to picnic or go for a swim. The grouping of trees kept them hidden from view off Lake Shore Drive, and the lake out in front of them afforded a natural barrier.

"See? What did I tell you?" Scott announced. "This is the perfect spot."

Alyssa looked around them with a guarded expression. "It is out of the way. No doubt about it." She hesitated a moment, then nodded. "But it's a good choice. We can eat our lunch, then maybe take a walk down the beach."

"Or even go for a swim," Libby added, patting the handbag at her side. "I'm glad I remembered to pack my suit."

Scott eyed the bag. She fit a swimsuit in there? He swallowed. There couldn't be much to it if she'd managed to find room in her small bag. He tried to avoid looking at Libby, but his traitorous eyes gave her a quick once-over. Maybe he should stay with the carriage and the picnic supplies if she decided to swim.

"And what about you, Alyssa? Did you pack your suit as well?"

Alyssa shook her head. "No, but there's nothing saying a barefoot walk along the beach wouldn't afford the same level of refreshment."

Scott snapped his fingers and pointed at her. "Exactly."

And bare feet were a much safer alternative to the bare skin Libby was sure to put on display. Oh, if only he'd thought to call Ben and invite him to join them. Then, he might not feel so outnumbered, or so out of his element. Maybe he could send Ben a text when the ladies weren't looking. Just what was Miss Edith thinking, sending him off with two beautiful ladies to share a lunch?

"So, how did you find this place?" Libby wanted to know.

Scott jerked his gaze to her and stuttered. "Oh, um, I bike a lot on this road. One day, I happened to stop here and discovered the natural alcove created by the trees. Seemed like a good place for our impromptu picnic."

At least it wasn't a lie. He did often ride his bike up this way. But, they didn't need to know his family owned the land across the drive behind them in the northwest corner of the island. Or that he'd known about this place from years of living just a few hundred feet away for most of his life.

Alyssa reached for an apple, took a juicy bite, and stared out at the lake. She shifted her focus and regarded her apple as if it held some special secret. "It is nice and private."

Her voice was so soft he had to strain to hear her above the lapping of the water against the shoreline. What in the last twenty minutes had made her retreat inside of herself so much?

"Hey, Lys," Libby called. "Snap out of it, will ya? We're supposed to be enjoying our vacation, remember?"

Well, whatever it was, Libby had obviously noticed it, too. And it had started right after they'd said good-bye to Miss Dottie. Wait! She must be fretting over what she'd learned about Miss Edith and the quilting group. Because the look on her face when Dottie told the story was nothing but surprise.

"I'm sorry, Lib." Alyssa reached down and ran her fingers through the sand, letting the granules slip through her fingers. "You're right."

Scott took a chance and reached out to touch her shoulder. She immediately turned her head to trace a visual line from his hand to his face. "I know what Miss Dottie said got to you, but remember, it's been sixteen years since it happened. I'm sure the hurt has long since faded."

"Or if not," Libby chimed in. "Your grandmother has at least been able to move past it and focus on more important things."

Alyssa tossed her apple core into a plastic bag and dumped it into the basket and then waved her hands out in front of her. "All right, all right, you two. No need to gang up on me." She reached for her insulated cup and pushed back the plastic piece over the opening.

He grinned. "Besides, if Miss Edith knew you were worrying about her right now, she'd probably find a way to dump a bucket of fresh lake water over your head."

Her lips tightened, preventing the lemonade she'd just drunk from escaping.

Scott laughed and placed his hands in his lap as he attempted to school his expression into one of nonchalance. It was no use. "I'm sorry," he said through barely contained chuckles. "I appreciate you sparing me the spray of your drink, though."

With a swallow and dainty clearing of her throat, Alyssa once again regained her composure. "You're welcome," she replied, raising her cup again to her mouth. "But I can't guarantee you'll remain free from harm if it happens again."

It took Scott a moment to process what she'd just said. He narrowed his eyes at the playful, underlying threat laced between her words. She spoke with such calm, her expression devoid of any mischief. He couldn't tell if she was flirting or serious. And she likely preferred it that way. Such a unique blend of distant politeness and affability.

He reached into the basket and retrieved the three overflowing sandwiches in individual ziploc bags. After handing one to each of the ladies, he stared at the overstuffed bread.

Holding it up for inspection, he raised his eyebrows and grinned. "Well? What do you think?"

"About your sense of humor or the made-with-care masterpieces my grandmother sent along with us?" She pulled her main meal from the ziploc bag and took a bite, the corners of her mouth turning up slightly as she chewed.

"My—" He paused. Had she just given him a taste of his own medicine? He clenched his jaw and raised his chin a fraction of an inch. "The sandwich, of course."

Alyssa swallowed and took another drink. "In this case, I approve. Then again, I've always known my grandmother is an amazing cook."

Libby laughed through her nose, and she pressed her lips together so hard, they turned white. "Didn't I say you ain't seen nothing yet when it came to Lys's wit?"

"Yes, you did." Only he'd never expected something like this.

"Whoa! What is in this lemonade?" Libby spun off the lid and peered at the liquid inside.

A full smile spread across Alyssa's face. "Another one of Grandma's special recipes. Lemon juice, sugar dissolved in hot water, mint leaves, a mixture of ice water and sparkling water, and lemon wheels to garnish."

Libby took another drink. "Mmm, it's delicious."

"Of course it is." Alyssa's chin went up a notch, as if the recipe was one of her own making. "Just like her sandwiches."

Scott leaned back against the trunk of the tree and regarded Alyssa. "I guess, other than her lemonade, I haven't been lucky enough to taste your grandmother's mouth-pleasing fare." Taking a bite of the ham, turkey, cheese, tomatoes, pickles, lettuce, and mustard between the bread, he released an exaggerated groan. "Mmm. It's the best sandwich I've ever had."

Alyssa covered her mouth and giggled. "And if you're like most other bachelors, probably the first homemade sandwich in a long while."

Scott shook a finger in her direction. "Not true. I seem to recall my mother making some when I was a boy." And he'd shared some with Caroline when they'd gone on picnics like this one. Whoa! Where had that thought come from? No. He wasn't going there. It would spoil what was, up to this moment, a perfect day.

Alyssa looked up at him again. She grinned, showing no sign that she sensed any of his inner turmoil. "And since then," she continued off his last response, "you've likely taken your fill of whatever was convenient."

He propped himself on one elbow. "I'll have you know our cook prepares delicious meals, and when I dine with my family, she makes sure each one of us eats some of everything she's made."

Alyssa paused with her sandwich midway to her mouth and stared. "You have a cook?" she managed, her voice thick.

"Yeah," Libby chimed in. "I thought you lived above your carriage house or in one of the staff cottages or apartments at the Grand."

Oh no! How was he going to get out of this one? Go for the nonchalant approach. It should work.

"Well, I do," he said, falling back on both elbows. "Live above my carriage house, that is. But our cook lives with my parents and is basically part of the family. Cooking is how she pays for the room my parents rent to her. And mmm, can she cook!"

Alyssa cocked her head and remained silent for several moments. Scott could feel the heat warm his neck and creep toward his ears. If either one of them figured out his family employed a butler and maidservants, there'd be no end to the long line of questions they'd ask.

"Makes sense," Alyssa finally said with a nod. "My own parents rented out their extra bedrooms when we kids moved out. They didn't want to sell their home, but they didn't want the rooms sitting empty either."

Scott didn't dare offer anything more. He might give away just how close they were to his family's property and the expensive homes on it. Time to get the focus off of him. Just as he opened his mouth to speak, Libby beat him to it.

"All right, I'm going to swim," she announced, eyeing them both in turn. "Either of you care to join me?"

"Lib, you already know I didn't pack my suit."

Scott sat up and raised his hands. "Neither did I."

Libby sighed and shook her head. "You two are such spoilsports. I can't believe you didn't come better prepared." She rolled her eyes. "Okay, I guess I'll just have to keep company with the fish and rocks."

"Or, I could join you," Ben announced, walking his bike toward them and propping it against a nearby tree. The grin he wore would put an impish grade-school boy to shame.

"Ben!" Libby beamed a wide smile. "At last. I won't have to go swimming alone after all."

"Nope." Ben swung two towels from over his shoulder and pinched a bit of his swim trunks. "And I came prepared, too," he added with nod at Scott.

"Just let me go change." After retrieving a suit in need of additional material, Libby sauntered off in the direction of some closely set trees.

Ben's gaze followed Libby, but he managed to tear it away from her, retreating back long enough to glance down at Scott and Alyssa. "Thanks for the text, pal." He glanced back over his shoulder then returned his attention to them. "Looks like I'm going to take a long lunch today. I owe you one."

"Anytime," Scott replied. Of course, he wasn't about to say the debt was being repaid right now with Ben occupying Libby. This way, he could call in the debt another time when it suited him.

"Ready!" Libby pushed through some branches and walked toward them to drop her bag next to Alyssa.

Scott raised an eyebrow. Yep. Just as he'd thought. Her suit was not all there. Ben whistled his appreciation and grinned down at Scott.

"I definitely owe you one." Ben shed his shirt and reached out to take Libby's hand. "Let's go."

"Hey, Ben!" When his friend turned around, Scott tossed him a tube of sun lotion. "Don't forget this."

Ben caught it, looked down at it, then waggled his eyebrows. "Oh yeah, this'll come in real handy."

Scott shook his head. Ben was always the comic and player. The pair took off toward the water's edge, disappearing to the right once they reached the sand. All right. So, he'd go to the left. And now was as good a time as ever.

Popping the final bit of sandwich into his mouth, Scott took a swig of lemonade to chase it down, sat up, and brushed his hands on his slacks, then stood. He stowed his cup in the basket and grabbed an apple, polishing it on his shirt before tossing it in the air to his left hand.

Alyssa shielded her eyes and looked up at him. This had to work. He smiled down at her and extended his right hand in her direction. She regarded it with a quizzical expression.

"So, how about that barefooted walk?"

7

Alyssa looked toward the lake, at the spot where Ben and Libby had just disappeared. Then she angled her chin to look up at Scott again. Had he planned this whole thing? Ben had mentioned a text Scott had sent, but she didn't recall seeing him with his phone since they'd arrived for their picnic. Still, the whole thing reeked of intentional orchestration. All so he could be alone with her.

She should be flattered. But as she stared at Scott's outstretched hand, waiting for her to accept his invitation, her heart hammered away inside her chest. Could she do this? She hadn't been alone with a guy in fourteen years, and it had ended on a sour note. But she couldn't let him stand there forever.

"I'd love to," Alyssa said, allowing him to help her to her feet. With her free hand, she dusted off the sandwich crumbs from her capris. Moving her hand to his shoulder and using him for balance, she kicked off her sandals then nudged them with her toes back onto the blanket.

Without leaning on her at all, Scott bent to remove his and did the same. "Ready?"

"As I'll ever be," she replied.

As they started walking, Scott placed his hand at the small of her back. And there went her hammering heartbeat again. She took several long breaths in an attempt to slow it down. He didn't need to know how much his close proximity and touch affected her. Alyssa had to find something else to catch her attention, something other than the dangerously attractive man at her side. So far, this experience was a far cry from the last solo encounter she'd had with a guy.

If she were Libby, she could play it up and have Scott tagging along like a wayward child begging for the crumbs of her attention. But it wasn't her style at all. Not even close. And Libby didn't intentionally do it to the men she met. It just happened. At least, Scott didn't seem inclined to start up idle chatter. His silence led her back on the trail of why he'd arranged for this little stroll in the first place.

The cool sand in the shade felt wonderful between her toes, and the lapping water from the lakeshore beckoned her. She veered a little to the right in answer to the call.

"Wait just a sec," Scott said, and she stopped as he bent and rolled up the legs of his pants.

Alyssa tried not to stare at the muscular definition in his calves. Strong legs had always appealed to her, though she wasn't sure why. Maybe the thought of a solid foundation made them attractive. Maybe the fact her lanky older brother had twigs for legs and loved to show them off caused her to seek out whatever didn't remind her of his spindly appendages. Whatever the reason, Scott's legs held her attention.

He straightened again, and she diverted her focus in the opposite direction. "There. Now we can head for the water. Just going to have to make it through the hot, dry sand first." Scott nodded toward her feet. "By the way, I like your anklet."

Alyssa didn't have to look to conjure up a picture of the delicate piece of jewelry surrounding her right ankle. Two hearts with a diamond in the center of each, connected to a simple cross in the middle, and a thin chain all the way around. "It was a gift from my father when I turned thirteen. His version of a purity ring, I suppose." And a promise she'd kept since she'd first linked the clasp. Though one incident had nearly destroyed it.

The thought returned unbidden, and she quickly shoved it back into the recesses of her mind where it belonged. The memory of the betrayal wouldn't invade this beautiful day. She wouldn't let it.

"Ready to make a run for it?"

Scott's question invaded her thoughts and got her focused back on the present. Without asking, he grabbed her hand and tugged her toward the lakeshore. The sting of the hot sand only hit for a second with each step, but she didn't want to get burned on the bottom of her feet either.

As soon as their feet touched the cooler, wet sand, they both expelled their breaths.

Scott laughed and looked back at the path they'd made. "It wasn't so bad."

"Not at all." Alyssa twisted her leg back and forth to drive her foot deeper into the mushy substance, letting the gelatinous liquid ooze between her toes. Next came the water. It crept onto the shore and receded like the rhythmic motion of one of those fifty-cent kiddie rides found at the mall or grocery store. When the water lapped at her feet, she pranced away. Then, almost immediately, she took a step further in, each step bringing the water higher toward her ankles.

Scott followed along, slipping his hands into his pockets as they inched their way along the shoreline.

"Is it just the way you remember it from years ago?"

Alyssa jerked to a stop and whipped her head around to stare at him. "How do you know I used to come here when I was younger?"

A sheepish grin appeared as he ducked his head a little. "Your grandmother and I have shared a few conversations when I'm giving her rides." He shrugged. "Guess some details have slipped out from time to time."

"Oh."

It certainly made sense. But Alyssa didn't like the idea of Grandma telling stories about her, especially not to a man who'd been a stranger to her until they'd met yesterday. Sort of gave him an edge in their conversation. And it left her wondering just how much Grandma had said about her.

"Don't worry," Scott said, pulling one hand out of his pocket as if to wave off her concerns. "I promise I don't believe all of it," he added with a grin.

Against her better judgment, she returned the grin. Might as well keep things lighthearted and safe. "Good, because in case you haven't noticed, Grandma can weave a yarn rather well. Her quilts aren't the only things to contain stories."

"So," he drew out the word, sounding cautious, "you did or you didn't come here every summer with your father?"

"Oh, I did," she replied. "Daddy grew up here and met Mom on the island. At the Grand Hotel in fact." Alyssa smiled as the memories of sitting on her father's knee and hearing him tell the story came rushing to the forefront of her mind. "I remember him saying how fate brought him and Mom together."

Scott's hand found its way to the small of her back again. "How so?" he asked, facing forward.

"Have you ever seen the movie *Somewhere in Time*?"

He nodded. "With Jane Seymour and Chris Reeve?" He chuckled. "Or Superman, as I like to call him."

"Yes."

"I'm familiar with it. The movie was filmed here."

"Back in 1979," she replied. "I know."

"And the hotel hosts this convention thing every year in October for the fans of the movie." Scott waved his hand in dismissal. "They get all dolled up, have some sort of promenade thing, reenact some scene down by the water, watch the movie, the works." He shrugged. "Last year, one of the ladies said something about the movie being a cult classic or something."

"Oh, it is! I've often wished I could come up and take part, but each year passes by, and I don't make it." She sighed. "I belong to INSITE, but I guess I don't make it enough of a priority."

"Insight? What's that?"

"It's the International Network of Somewhere in Time Enthusiasts."

Scott regarded her with a raised eyebrow. "I take it you're a card-carrying member?"

She giggled. "Almost. They don't have membership cards, but I do pay dues each year for the quarterly magazine with all the news from the club."

Scott bent and picked up a stone then winged it toward the water. "So, what does all of it have to do with your parents?"

"Their names are Richard and Elise."

Scott stopped and turned to face her. "You're kidding."

Alyssa grinned and shook her head. "Not in the least."

He narrowed his eyes and pressed his lips together. "If you tell me there's a Collier or McKenna in your family somewhere, I might have to go to your grandmother and ask for proof."

Ah, so he'd obviously seen the movie or knew enough about it to know the principal characters' names. Then again, he did work at the Grand. Maybe it was required viewing for all employees or something.

"Close," she finally said. "My middle name is McKenna. And the film is one of my all-time favorites."

He started walking again. "Alyssa McKenna Denham." The corners of his mouth quirked. "Has a nice ring to it."

She squared her shoulders. "I like to think so."

"All right, so your parents share the same names as Seymour and Reeve's characters in the movie, and they gave you your middle name in honor of the lead in the film." He glanced down at her. "Is it why your father brought you back here so often?"

"Partially." She'd save the way she'd begged to see the horses for later. "And also because he loved this island so much. He wanted to share it with me."

The pressure from Scott's hand increased. "Your grandmother told me about your father's sickness. I'm sorry."

"Thank you." Alyssa closed her eyes and willed away the fresh wave of pain. *Lord, please get me through this, and maybe turn the conversation to something a little less personal.* "I was just about to turn fifteen when the cancer was discovered. Grandpa had died the year before of the same thing. They tried to treat it, but it grew too fast. Before Christmas, he was gone." She blinked several times and inhaled a ragged breath. "It's been almost fifteen years, but at times, it feels like yesterday."

A lone tear escaped and raced down her cheek. Scott reached across and caught it with his finger. They both stopped, and he tipped up her chin. She sniffed once and wet her lips. His gaze drifted to her mouth for a second or two before making its way back up to merge with hers.

"Hey," he said softly. "It's okay to cry. It must have been very hard and painful for you." He pivoted to face forward again and slipped his arm around her waist, this time gently coaxing her to resume walking. "No reason to bottle up your emotion. It'll only make it worse when it pops the cork and breaks free."

Alyssa wanted to ask what he meant, but she didn't. It sounded like he had his own story to tell of possible loss or pain. Maybe another time.

"But I've already shed enough tears to fill a river," she confessed.

"Then, let's talk about something else."

Yes, please. Anything but the sad memories. "Very well. What did you have in mind?"

For about fifteen or twenty feet, silence fell between them. Her brain blanked on anything to discuss. Not even an icebreaker came to mind. How exactly could she start a lighter topic in the wake of such a somber one?

Scott snapped his fingers. "I've got it."

Alyssa waited for this great idea he had.

"Where is home?" he finally said.

"Grand Rapids." Yes. Stick to the facts. She could answer those easily enough.

"And other than your grandmother, the rest of your family lives there, too?"

"Well, my mother does, and my older brother with his wife and three kids." The same niece and nephews had her mom pressuring her to provide a fourth grandchild. "In fact, all of Mother's family is in and around the western or southwestern part of the state. But all of Daddy's family is on the Upper Peninsula or here on the island."

He glanced down at her. "You mean, you have someone other than your grandmother living here?"

She nodded. "An uncle, yes." At least she thought he still lived there. Grandma hadn't mentioned otherwise. "But like Grandma, I haven't seen him since Daddy passed away."

"What's his name? Maybe I know him."

"Frederick."

"Frederick Denham. Fred Denham!" He slapped his thigh. "Yes, the one who owns the barber shop on Main."

All right, so Uncle Fred *did* still live on the island. "Yep."

Scott reached up and stroked his chin. "Been there a few times myself when my own attempt at personal grooming wasn't enough. Your uncle does good work." He bent and snatched another rock from the sand and winged it into the lake. Like the last one, it hit the water with a *kerplop* and sank.

Alyssa giggled. "You aren't trying to skip those rocks, are you? Because if you are, you're not doing a very good job of it."

He gave her a wry grin. "Did you have to state the obvious?"

She shrugged. "You know me. Libby told you last night I had a penchant for it."

"Yeah." He chuckled. "Well, I don't know if I'm attempting to skip them so much as just throwing the rocks back into the lake."

"Good, because the eroded rocks around here most likely wouldn't make desirable skipping stones. You need to find the ones made smooth by water, too." To prove her point, she retrieved one from the sand at their feet and traced an intricate pattern on its face. "The sand erosion makes these uneven tracks. The ones in the water are what you need." Alyssa rolled the rock around in her hand. "These have fissures created by the friction of the sand on the surface. Like selective exfoliation."

A half-chuckle, half-chortle came out of Scott's mouth. "You mean, like a facial?"

"Yes, only it's been performed in specific areas on the surface and not all over."

"That would make for one rough-looking lady."

An image formed of a woman with stripes on her face from a microdermabrasion treatment, and she laughed. "Yes, I suppose it would."

Scott paused and looked back over his shoulder. "Uh, do you think maybe we should be getting back?"

Honestly? No. She'd rather keep on walking and learning more about what Grandma had told this man. But he was right. They had been gone a little while.

"Ben and Libby are likely out of the water by now," he continued, scanning the horizon.

"And probably wondering where we've gone." Or maybe enjoying the extra time together without her and Scott to crowd them.

Scott made a slow turn on his heel toward the direction from which they'd come and extended his left arm toward her. Alyssa fell in step with him, though the excitement of the walk had dimmed considerably.

"We'll have to do this again, only without the daring duo chaperones."

Alyssa glanced up, but Scott kept his gaze straight ahead, his face devoid of any discernible emotion. Was he asking her out? Or was he just being polite? No, if so, he wouldn't have mentioned the lack of chaperones. So, yes. It was a date. Sort of. And a safe enough one Alyssa wouldn't mind repeating.

"Yes, we should," she replied.

He grinned down at her. "How about we make plans when I drive you and Libby to the next stop on your quilting adventure?"

Alyssa did a quick mental calculation. It would be on Thursday. Yes, it could work. "Sure. We can talk about the details then."

"Great." Scott nodded out in front of them. "Looks like some-one's been waiting for us."

Two people who looked like Ben and Libby jumped up and down on the beach ahead of them, waving their arms. Did they think they needed to signal her and Scott? As if they couldn't find their way back to the carriage on their own? It wasn't like the beach was extensive, and there weren't many options for getting lost. Of course, if they could, she might consider it, simply to extend her time with Scott.

Oh well, at least she could look forward to Thursday.

"You know," Ben said as he hefted his bike from the back of the carriage. "If I didn't know better, I'd think you sent me the text earlier so *you* could take your walk, not to give *me* solo time with Libby."

Scott shrugged as he unhitched his horse and backed the carriage away. "It all worked out, didn't it?" Better than he'd expected, actually.

"Yep." Ben flipped his bike upside down and inspected the wire connection to the gears. "Libby and I had a lot of fun swimming." He stood and walked to the toolbox just inside the carriage garage. "Even talked some about you and Alyssa."

Scott dropped the bar, and it hit the pavement with a metallic clang. "You did what?"

One of his caretakers came to lead the horse away, and Scott nodded his thanks. He did a one-eighty turn to face his friend, but Ben didn't look up. He just kept working on his bike, twisting and tightening and adjusting.

"We talked about you two." Finally, Ben raised his gaze, and a slow grin spread across his face. "And let me tell you, Libby had a few interesting things to share about her friend."

"Such as?"

"Wouldn't you like to know?"

Scott growled low in his throat. "Come on, Ben. Spill it, will ya?" He marched over to where Ben squatted and yanked the wrench out of his hand. "You know I never like it when you play your games."

Ben snatched the wrench back. "I was using this."

"Well, you better get to the point," he said, ramming his fists onto his hips. "Or I'm gonna close up shop and you can find some other place to mooch tools."

"Touchy, aren't we?" He again went back to working on his bike. "The little gal must have gotten under your skin more than I thought."

"My opinion of Alyssa doesn't matter right now."

"Actually, it might, once you hear what I heard today."

Scott took three steps backward and leaned against the outside wall of his shop. This was getting aggravating fast. He folded his arms across his chest and glared at Ben. "Well? I haven't got all day." He glanced down at his watch. "And speaking of which, shouldn't you be getting back to the hotel?" His friend didn't need another excuse to drag out this supposedly earth-shattering information he had.

"Nope. Ms. Bloswick gave me the afternoon off since I'll be pulling a double shift tomorrow."

"Double shift?" Great. So Ben wasn't in a hurry to get anywhere. "For what?"

"Offered to work for Steve, remember?" Ben looked up again and raised his eyebrows. "So he could head back to the mainland and visit his grandfather in the hospital?"

"And Hulett was okay with it?" Their managing director could be quite the stickler for employee alertness, and double shifts didn't usually fall within the allowable scale.

"He didn't have much say in the matter. Bloswick's the general manager, remember? Hulett answers to her."

All right. Enough of this aimless talk about their superiors. Scott had at least six to eight other things he could be doing right now. He just wanted this conversation over and done.

"Right," he said. "So, back to your talk with Libby this afternoon." Scott pushed off the wall and looked again at his watch. "You've got exactly fifteen seconds to start talking, or I'm going back to work, and I'll find out from someone else." Like somehow asking Libby himself, or even getting Alyssa to tell him.

"All right, all right. Just hold your horses." He waved his hand in the general direction of the stables. "Oh, wait. You can't. You've already let him go."

Scott clenched his teeth. "Benjamin Webster, you're now down to five seconds."

His friend's chuckle grated on his nerves, but at least his threat seemed to work.

"Sheesh." Ben stood and flipped his bike right-side up. "Some people just can't take a joke." He grabbed the handle and leaned his weight against the bike, crossing one ankle over the other. "Seems our little contest winner is quite familiar with this island. In fact, she's been here many times before."

Scott groaned again. What about something he didn't know? If this was all Ben had to share, so help him . . .

"Yes, I know," Scott said instead. "She spent every summer here growing up. Her dad brought her, and they stayed with her grandmother."

"Yes, but did you also know she stopped coming the summer after her dad died? And she hasn't been back here until yesterday?"

He wouldn't have if he hadn't heard it from Alyssa's own lips earlier this morning. Wow. Had it only been yesterday when she'd arrived?

"Yes, and yes," Scott said in response to Ben's two questions.

"Well, what if I told you the reason she stopped had nothing to do with her father?"

Now this was something he didn't expect. "What do you mean?"

Ben used the toe of his shoe to extend the kickstand, then leaned his bike down and used it partially as support as he crossed his arms in a mirror pose to Scott. "Well, Libby didn't know all the details, but she said something happened to Alyssa her last summer here. Something big. And she wouldn't tell anyone about it. Not even Libby."

It had to be big if she wouldn't even confide in her best friend. "So, how does Libby know anything happened?"

"Because she said Alyssa changed after her last visit. She was more withdrawn, more hesitant to go out and do things with Libby, all focused on her schoolwork and getting into college."

"I've known a lot of people who made the decision to shirk the fun and focus on studies at her age." He withdrew his right hand and rammed a thumb into his shoulder. "I was one of them."

"Well, yeah," Ben replied, extending his arm toward Scott, palm opened. "But you still went on dates and talked to a lot of girls." He grinned. "You might have disappointed a few when you didn't ask them out, but at least you still stayed on the radar. Alyssa wouldn't talk to or about guys at all. She wouldn't even let Libby fix her up on a blind date or introduce her to anyone." He gave Scott a pointed glance. "In fact, Libby says you're the first guy who isn't family who she's agreed to be alone with in nearly fourteen years."

Fourteen years? No way. Scott drew his eyebrows together. "Are you sure about this?"

Ben held up three fingers close together. "Scout's honor."

Scott let a grin tug at his mouth. "You were never a Scout."

"So? Neither were you." Ben grinned. "And it's not the point. The point is the little gal's got a heap of hurt or something weighing down on her, and you're the first guy she's let get close since whatever happened to her happened."

Wow. In his wildest imagination, he never would've come up with a story like this. There was a moment or two on their walk when he sensed she was holding back, but he had no idea it was this big. And he didn't even know the source of this "big" thing.

"Hey." Ben's hand on his shoulder interrupted his musings. "I told you it was important."

"Yeah." Scott sighed. "You weren't kidding . . . for a change."

"And I know this isn't easy for you." He squeezed Scott's arm. "Seeing how much she looks like Caroline and all."

Scott closed his eyes. Now why did Ben have to go and mention her? He'd just learned he might be the only one who could get Alyssa to open up, but if he did, she might turn on him the way Caroline had. And where would it leave him? Scott couldn't go through that again.

He reached up and scrubbed his face with both hands, groaning. "I'm no good at this." Lowering his hands, he looked at Ben.

"Why couldn't it be you? Why couldn't she have opened up to you instead?"

"Because she didn't see me. She saw you," he pointed out. "And there's obviously a greater plan in all of this."

"I just wish I would've been let in on it before it was dumped in my lap."

"Look, Scott." Ben gave him a punch on the arm. "You've got this. It's been almost two years since Caroline left. And now another beautiful gal walks into your life, who obviously needs you." He took a step back and turned toward his bike. Another step, and he grabbed hold of the handlebars, kicking the kickstand back into position. "Don't let this one get away."

Scott snorted. As if he'd run Caroline off on purpose. Or would intentionally jeopardize whatever this was with Alyssa.

Ben swung his leg over his bike seat and looked again at Scott. "Well, I've done my part. The rest is up to you."

As Ben rode away, Scott stared off to the right and looked through the trees toward the southeast shore of the island. Yes, the rest was up to him. But how was he going to face Alyssa again knowing what he knew? And how was he going to keep her from realizing it?

8

Alyssa slipped the list of quilting bee names into the pouch, draped the flap over the opening, and snapped the pouch shut. Three down, seven to go. And it was only Thursday.

"Oh, this quilt is already taking shape." Grandma held the squares already collected against the blue backing she'd selected. "It's going to be beautiful once it's complete."

"A true masterpiece," Alyssa agreed. "And if today goes well, we'll have two more squares to add to the pile, and we'll be halfway there."

Grandma glanced around the main room of her cottage. "Speaking of 'we', where is your Siamese twin this morning?"

"Oh, she decided to stay back at the hotel today and take in some of those enticing activities the brochure promised her." And Alyssa couldn't fault her. Assembling this quilt didn't have anything to do with Libby. "I told her to have fun. She deserved it."

"It was nice of you." Grandma folded the backing neatly and laid it across her sofa. "So, it will be just you and Scott then on these two visits?"

"Whenever he arrives," Alyssa replied. "Yes."

"It's a nice change of pace." She sighed. "He's such a polite young man."

Grandma's voice sounded a little off. Alyssa peered across the room at her, waiting for her to glance her way, but Grandma didn't. Instead, she busied herself with arranging an immaculate desk and fluffing out plump pillows. She was definitely up to something.

"Grandma . . ."

"Yes, dear?" Grandma finally looked up from the other side of the couch, and her entire face held more mischief than the Cheshire cat.

"Have you said something to Scott to lead him to believe there might be a chance for something between us?" Scott said Grandma had told him about her. Just how much had she revealed?

"And risk a rift in our rekindled relationship? No, dear, I haven't." Not a hint of deception showed on her face, and Alyssa believed her. "I might have shared a few things about you in a general manner, but it was merely a simple conversation between friends." Grandma moved around the couch and walked toward Alyssa. "Nothing more, I promise." She brushed her knuckles across Alyssa's cheek. "I would never think of doing anything like that to you."

Alyssa leaned into her grandmother's hand and smiled. "I know. But you were acting so strangely a moment ago, I had to ask."

The trill of the phone interrupted anything further, and Grandma reached to answer it.

"Oh, is everything all right?" she asked after several moments.

Grandma held up a finger, just as Alyssa took a step toward her. Who was on the phone? And what had happened? Maybe it was Scott. Alyssa glanced out the front window. No sign of a carriage or her escort. Oh, she hoped nothing had happened to him.

"Yes, yes. I understand. I'll tell her." She paused. "And I hope you're able to get everything rearranged for this weekend." The other voice buzzed through the phone. "And you do the same. Thank you for calling. Good-bye."

"Well?" Alyssa asked as soon as Grandma hung up. "Who was it? And what did they have to say?"

Grandma pressed her lips into a thin line. "As you have no doubt surmised, it was Scott, and he won't be making it to escort you this morning after all."

"Is he all right?" The call hadn't sounded urgent, but a one-sided conversation could only reveal so much. *Please, God, let him be fine.*

"Yes, he's fine. But an emergency came up at the hotel, and they put out an APB on all available staff to report to their duty stations. A wedding not supposed to take place until next weekend is actually happening this weekend, instead."

Alyssa gasped. "Can they do that? Does the hotel even allow such a thing this close to an event?"

"Under normal circumstances, no, but this is the governor's daughter, and you simply do not say no to him."

"Hmm, wonder what happened to make them move it up. You'd think with a wedding this size, the wedding coordinator would have everything under control."

"I'm sure it'll all work out." Grandma handed Alyssa another insulated cup of lemonade. "In the meantime, you've got some places to go and people to see." She smiled. "There's a nice bike in the shed on the side of the house. It's not a horse-drawn carriage with a handsome driver," she said with a grin. "But it'll suffice."

"Grandma? Why don't you come with me today?" The idea had just popped into Alyssa's head. And it was perfect. "We can call Scott's shop and see if they can send another driver, or we can call one of the other services on the island."

Some of the color drained from Grandma's face, and she turned away to busy herself with moving a small stack of papers over to her desk. "No, no," she replied after several moments, her voice thick. "You go on." She took a deep breath, touched the silver crown of hair upon her head, and turned to face Alyssa. "I have a hair appointment at eleven, and if I miss it, I'll have to reschedule. It might be weeks before I can get in again."

Something wasn't right. The slight frown and the sudden lines on her grandmother's forehead didn't fit.

"Are you sure? It wouldn't be any trouble to call another carriage."

Grandma nodded once. "I'm certain. I've gotten rather set in my ways lately, and if Scott isn't available, I either walk, or I don't go anywhere."

Alyssa smiled. Stubborn as a mule. But it's why most people loved her. She turned her stubbornness into persistence when she wanted something accomplished, and one way or another, she got it done.

She returned to stand in front of Alyssa and made a shooing motion toward the front door. "Now, be off with you."

Alyssa laughed. "Are you trying to get rid of me?" Or maybe trying to avoid sharing what was on her mind.

Grandma gave her a quick hug. "Never, dear." She tapped the pouch. "But Judith and Betty might not be around all morning. So, you'd better get moving."

"All right."

After a quick kiss on her Grandma's cheek, Alyssa headed outside to the shed to retrieve her transportation for the day. The conversation with Grandma was far from over. Grandma had a reason for not wanting to accompany her on these visits. But she couldn't avoid the issue forever.

Judith. The neatly penned name filled the fourth slot on her list. Alyssa looked up at the white and stone Victorian perched on a hill above Main. She double-checked the address again. This was the right one. Next door to a charming bed-and-breakfast.

These island homes gave new meaning to the word *cottage*. If the stone wall and green iron perimeter fence at its base didn't command attention, then the beautiful landscaping designed with the bluff in mind would. Several shaped and groomed bushes adorned the lowest level of the cottage, and the wrap-around porch directly above had a white railing that held an American flag the same size as the ones flying from the Grand's front porch. Two gatherings of trees stood sentinel on either side of the home, a stunning picture against the backdrop of the vibrant blue sky.

"Well, here goes nothing," she muttered.

Alyssa leaned her bike against the interior side of one of the stone walls concealing the entrance to the home. With a deep breath, she took her first step of the four levels of stairs leading to the porch. Never let it be said she wasn't getting her exercise.

As soon as she reached the top, the screen door to the porch opened. "Alyssa Denham?" A well-dressed woman holding a tall glass of ice water greeted her.

"Yes," was all Alyssa could manage at the moment.

"Come in, child," the woman said, handing her the glass of water and stepping back to allow Alyssa to precede her. "You look as if you could use this."

"Thank you," Alyssa said, taking a drink and breathing a sigh of relief as the cold water washed down the dryness of her parched throat.

"Please, take a seat." The woman extended her hand toward any of three white wicker seats with coordinating cushions set against the outside screened wall. "My name is Judith Roebuck, and though I've heard a lot about you over the years, I don't believe we've officially met."

Alyssa searched her memory for the name or the face. "No, ma'am. I don't think so." She would have remembered a home like this if they had.

"Your grandmother speaks quite highly of you." She reached for her own glass of water and took a sip. "When I received her e-mail telling me you would be dropping by this morning, I made certain to clear my schedule."

"Oh!" Alyssa sat a little straighter. "Then, I won't keep you long."

"Nonsense." Judith waved off her concern. "I have at least thirty minutes until my next appointment," she added with a smile and a wink. "Please, relax. Take a few moments to catch your breath." She nodded in the direction of the street out front. "I know it's quite a walk up all those stairs. I often come in from the back entrance, but obviously not if I'm walking back from Main."

Alyssa glanced through the screen to see as much of the stairs as her vision allowed. "It is a lot of steps, but it's also a beautiful home. I can't imagine the cottage without the staircase. An inclined sidewalk or even basic stone steps wouldn't do it justice."

Judith raised her eyebrows. "You have a keen eye for detail, my dear. You don't happen to work in any sort of design field, do you? I know several businesses here on the island always looking for key designers for their teams."

It wasn't the first time someone had asked her that. But it was the first time anyone had mentioned employment on the island. Of course, if they could see her simple apartment back home, they'd wonder where the disconnect occurred. She laughed. "No. I have a business degree and work as an executive administrative assistant for a direct-selling company and product manufacturer just outside of Grand Rapids."

"Oh, too bad." She brightened. "Well, if you ever change your mind . . ."

Not likely. "I appreciate it, Mrs. Roebuck, but—"

"Judith, please," she replied, flattening her palm against her chest. "Edith and I go way back, and there's no need for such formalities among friends."

Alyssa nodded and let her shoulders fall a little. "Judith. And thank you for your vote of confidence, but I love my job, and as nice as it is here, I don't see me leaving it anytime soon."

Judith leaned back in her seat and raised her glass again to her lips. "Suit yourself," she said as she took a sip. Cushioning the glass in the palm of her other hand, she nodded toward Alyssa. "Now, why don't you tell me what Edith has sent you to say on her behalf."

Good. They were back on track. "Well, you mentioned receiving an e-mail from my grandmother."

"Yes. In fact, I read it just last night. And a good thing I did, too, or I might not have been here to greet you."

There she went again with her hectic schedule. Yet, she'd made it a point to clear it long enough for Alyssa to visit. And she was even later than planned thanks to the delay in leaving this morning. It said a lot about her friendship with Grandma.

"Tell me, Alyssa," Judith continued. "Do you know why Edith is not making these rounds herself to collect the blocks for the quilt?"

Well, this answered her question of whether or not Judith knew the purpose of her visit. "No, I don't." In fact, until this morning, she hadn't given it much thought. Just considered it a nice gesture she could do for Grandma after deserting her all those years ago.

"I've tried to include her in several social engagements here on the island, and I've even phoned during my free time to see if she'd be up for a visit." The corners of her mouth turned down, and tiny lines formed near the bridge of her nose. "Every time, Edith has one excuse or another as to why she isn't available or why it's not a good time."

"Judith, I can honestly say I have no idea about her reasoning. When I called to tell her I was coming for a visit, she mentioned this quilt project to me and asked if I'd like to help." Alyssa shrugged. "It sounded like a fun adventure to add to the two weeks' vacation and other activities the hotel was providing, so I agreed."

Like night to day, Judith's expression brightened, and she sat forward. "Wait, are you the one who won the essay contest the Grand sponsored? The one from the bridal magazine?"

Alyssa closed her eyes. Here it goes again. She should've known the news would travel fast on an island only one and a half miles at its widest point. "Yes," she said as she opened her eyes. "And I brought the friend who dared me to enter it along for the fun."

"You mean you were looking in a bridal magazine, and you aren't even engaged?" Judith set down her drink on the table and clapped her hands together once, pulling them in toward her chest. "Oh, this is delightful."

Delightful? It wasn't a word Alyssa would use to describe the entire debacle. Humiliating, pathetic, and maybe even laughable. But definitely not delightful.

"It appears your grandmother and you have a lot more in common than you might think."

"Oh?" She'd heard she resembled her grandmother in appearance, but how could prematurely flipping through a bridal catalog link her to Grandma? "What makes you say so?"

"Because when we were young girls, we spent a lot of time poring over Sears catalogs, dreaming of the items we'd love to buy but couldn't afford at the time." She sighed. "With a country just having gone through the Depression and then almost immediately entering the Second World War, funds and the availability of getting more of them were at an all-time low." A smile widened her mouth. "But your grandmother, bless her heart, she wouldn't let it get her down."

Yep. It sounded like Grandma. Alyssa scooted forward on her chair. "What did she do?"

"She took scissors and cut out the items she dearly wanted, the ones atop her list of desires, and she glued them together in a precise collage of sorts, sticking the organized collection of random things on her wall where she could look at it every day and dream." The distasteful expression on Judith's face and the way she spoke made it seem like Grandma's chosen method of inspiration didn't suit her friend.

"Well, they do say to put your dreams in front of you where you won't forget about them or get distracted from them by other things," Alyssa pointed out.

"Yes, but she could have organized them a little more neatly." Judith's chin raised a half-inch. "Maybe even gotten a book or something so she could put each item on its own page and cross it off once she had it."

Now this sounded more like the grandmother she knew today. Maybe Judith's influence had changed her. "But then Grandma would have to flip through each and every page to see all of the items she wanted." Alyssa shrugged. "This way, she could see everything at once."

Judith chuckled. "You, my dear, are exactly like her. Thought process and all." She held up one finger. "But I bet you wouldn't go so far as to ask the store owners or the manufacturers themselves if they had used versions of the items they were willing to give away to her or sell cheap."

Alyssa covered her mouth and giggled. "Grandma did that?" Oh, the things she had yet to learn about her endearing grandmother. "But how did she know the manufacturers?"

"Well, in case you haven't noticed my last name, dear. It's Roebuck. As in—"

Alyssa gasped. "Sears & Roebuck!" No wonder she lived in such a beautiful home.

"And Company," Judith added with a nod. "And the 'company' part happens to include my branch of the family tree as well. My husband's great-uncle was Alvah Roebuck, the watchmaker from Indiana who partnered with Richard Sears back in the 1880s." Pride oozed out with her words. "And your dear, sweet grandmother got it into her fanciful head it would be both economical and shrewd to seek out discounted wares instead of waiting to save up the money and buy the brand new ones herself." She shook her head with an amused grin. "Since my family had direct stock in the catalogs and business agreements with those who made or sold the products they advertised, she targeted us."

"It all sounds like such an outrageous tale, but knowing my grandmother the way I do, I can see how it might be possible."

"Believe me, Alyssa, I could tell you stories of your grandmother from when we were younger." Judith grinned. "But I'm not certain she would appreciate you learning some of those things about her." She winked. "At least not without her present."

Alyssa smiled. "Ah, yes, so she can verify the facts."

Judith tapped her index finger in the air. "Exactly."

Church bells pealed from somewhere close by, likely from St. Anne's Catholic Church down the street.

Judith looked down at her watch. "Mercy me! I completely lost track of the time." She stood, and Alyssa did the same. "Before you go, let me get you the block for Edith's quilt." After grabbing her glass, she headed for the front door to her home. "What a travesty it would be for you to come all this way and leave without the whole purpose of your coming," she said as she disappeared inside.

Alyssa turned to stare out from the porch over the rooftops of the buildings across Main and toward the crystal-blue lake. From this vantage point, she could see the stone wall barriers off the southern points of the island. Yachts in every shape and size were docked in front of Mackinac Yacht Club, and other boats roamed around the bay. The dock where Scott and Ben had brought her and Libby on Monday jutted out from around the curve of the road. Hard to believe only three days had passed since then.

"Here we are!" Judith announced, pushing through the interior screen door and letting it swing back with a clap of wood on wood. She walked up to Alyssa and presented the block with a flourish. "For Edith's grand quilt, my dear."

Alyssa took it and looked down, then chuckled. There, in the center were two replica Sears catalogs and a gold pocket watch stitched in the midst of a light blue background with cranberry and daffodil accents.

"Oh, Grandma is going to love this one."

"I wish I could be there to see her face when you show it to her." She again glanced at her watch. "But alas, duty calls. And I must be on my way."

"Yes, and I have another stop to make myself."

Judith extended her arm out toward Alyssa and silently encouraged her to walk with her. "Alyssa, I have loved every minute of our little chat." When they reached the outside screen door, she turned. "Please, tell your grandmother how much I miss seeing her and how much I wish we could get together in person to catch up. E-mail is nice, but there's nothing like seeing her face to face."

"I will, Judith. I promise." Alyssa slipped the square into her pouch and reached for the handle to the door. "Thank you again for the water and the stories."

And now for the stairs. Alyssa took another deep breath. At least she was going down this time and not up.

The next home looked nothing like the cottages on the bluffs. In fact, it resembled an estate she'd find on the west side of Grand Rapids. She should have been approaching this house in a private carriage instead of riding up on a personal bicycle. After traveling nearly all the way up Hoban Avenue and turning onto 7th Street, she'd followed the road around to where it became Trillium Drive. The GPS on her cell phone had showed the house at the end of the street, so she rode until she reached the driveway.

A three-car garage sat off to her right, attached to the house by a wing. Beautifully landscaped lawns extended behind her and around to her left with a sizeable shed to the left of the home. The house itself sat in the middle of several tall trees appearing to have had their lower branches removed, making them look like green sticks of cotton candy. And the square footage of the place must have topped four thousand. The front patio alone with its three columns supporting the overhang was bigger than her living room and dining room combined.

After swinging her leg around, Alyssa walked her bike toward the house and passed under a roof connecting four pillars at the corners that could have served as a guardhouse or something. But a guard wasn't on duty today, so she kept on walking, following the curved driveway around to the front of the house. She leaned her bike against one of the patio pillars and stepped toward the main door.

Before she could knock, the door opened, and a sour-looking woman with pinched lips and steely black eyes stared through the screen.

"May I help you?" she greeted. If she could even call it a greeting. Certainly not a welcoming one.

"Yes, my name is Alyssa Denham, and I'm here on behalf of my grandmother, Edith Denham, to see Betty Clingerman. Is she at home?"

"No, I'm sorry. Mrs. Clingerman is not available for visitors at this time. Are you here to collect the block for the quilt your grandmother is putting together?"

Well, Betty might not be at home, but she had at least told her maid or housekeeper to expect her. "Yes. Do you happen to have it?" Alyssa didn't exactly want to make a repeat visit to this home.

The woman produced a manila envelope with Grandma's name scrawled on the front. "Yes. Mrs. Clingerman asked me to give this to you when you arrived." She opened the screen door just enough to slip the envelope to Alyssa, then shut it again and stood there staring as if she couldn't wait for Alyssa to leave.

"Thank you." Alyssa tucked it into her pouch. "And please tell Mrs. Clingerman I stopped by."

No response. No agreement. Not even a nod.

"Have a nice day!" At least, she could be polite even if the staff of the house wasn't. Alyssa couldn't get away from this place fast enough.

<hr />

Grandma was right. There were several bike racks behind the hotel, on the side of the carriage houses, and down the walk from the employee apartments. Assured everything was in order, she spun the dials on the lock a few times and then let the plastic-wrapped chain fall. Patting the pouch at her hip, she smiled. Not a bad day's work, if she did say so herself. And she had collected half of the squares on Grandma's list, plus learned a few things about some rather fascinating ladies. What would she discover from the other five women?

Alyssa ran her hand across the smooth lines of the bike and backed away, turning to walk toward the hotel . . . right into Charles Jarman.

Her hand went to her throat as it closed around her breath. Darkness encroached on the corners of her eyes, and the blood rushed from her face. His face, however, looked exactly the same. A little older and a bit more sinister, but still much the same as the boy she once knew. After all these years, she thought he would've left the island by now. He'd made no qualms about it not being his favorite place, and he only remained there to appease his family. Once he was of age, he'd be gone. So, why was he here? And why now?

"Charlie!" she croaked.

9

"Ah, if it isn't little miss Alyssa Denham, back on the island after all these years." Charlie crossed his arms and quirked one eyebrow, but a devilish expression on his face set Alyssa's heart jumping. Or maybe it was her inability to breathe properly. "I had wondered if the rumors I was hearing were true, so I decided to come and find out for myself." His mouth curled into a sardonic grin as he reached out and traced a finger down her cheek. "Looks like this little visit could be a memorable one for both of us."

She fought hard not to recoil at his touch. It would only encourage him even more. Alyssa looked to the left and the right. There had to be a way to escape somewhere. She knew enough about the hotel's property to at least make it to the porch, and there were always people milling about. Safety in numbers. If only she'd thought of it before she walked her bike to this secluded area behind the hotel.

"If you're looking for your precious Scott, he's otherwise engaged with the festivities coming this weekend. In case you hadn't heard, the governor's daughter is getting married." His voice had the schooled edge of trying too hard to appear nonchalant.

"How do you—"

"Know about Scott?" he finished for her. "Not much happens on this island I don't know about, my dear."

Coming from anyone else, the term of endearment would be welcome, but from Charlie? It only made the lunch she'd had not too long ago want to make a second appearance.

"For instance," Charlie said as he stepped closer and grabbed her arm. Alyssa turned her nose away from the overpowering scent of his cologne. "I even know about this idiotic thing you're doing with the quilt and the little picnic you and your Scott took two days ago."

"He's not my Scott," she said without thinking. Though at this moment, she'd give anything to see his face. "Only a friend who has offered his services in transportation."

"Ah, yes," he replied, his mouth curling without humor. "The kind Mr. Whitman. Escort and driver, and available for your every need."

Alyssa bristled at the innuendo. "I don't like what you're insinuating, Charlie. Scott's been nothing but a gentleman since the day we met. Which is more than I can say for you."

Charlie remained unaffected by her insult. "Now, is this any way to talk to someone just asking about your health?" he chided gently.

She must be careful. Something about his presence and demeanor suggested he was playing some sort of game, just like the last time she'd seen him. It's when he'd muttered something about her no longer having her chaperone present. And she could finally make decisions for herself. She could only assume he'd meant her father, as he was the only man with her at the time.

"My health is fine, Charlie, but I'm tired after the long morning."

"Then, why don't we go for a walk? I'd like to continue the conversation we had on the beach when you left me standing there and never returned."

The beach? Alyssa's gut tightened. Maybe she could use kindness to knock him off his game. It was better than the risk of angering him. "Thank you, but my head is pounding and my back aches. I would like nothing more than to rest." She started to step around him. "Please excuse me."

He released her elbow to grab her wrist, painfully stopping her departure, and pressed her against the carriage house wall. "This isn't exactly how you're supposed to respond."

"I'm sorry, but—"

"You don't need to apologize for the desire I see in your eyes, even if your lovely mouth says differently."

Alyssa's indignation hitched in her throat. How could she have ever trusted him, ever considered him a friend? Sure, somewhere back in their genealogy, they shared a relative, but—

"There's no reason to fear," he assured her. "I'm only going to make you realize what your eyes already know."

As he leaned toward her, Alyssa felt like a cornered animal, one who'd inadvertently invited capture. Backed up against the wall, there was nowhere to run.

As he lowered his head to hers, Alyssa inhaled his hot breath, ready to scream. No. No. Not again. Her past collided with her present in a crash of head-throbbing proportions. But before she could find her voice, Charlie rose off the ground, lifted by unseen hands, and whirled away. He stumbled over his own feet and grasped for one of the bike rack posts to keep from sprawling on the ground.

"Get away from her!"

Alyssa snapped her head away from her startled assailant to where Scott stood like a towering god of thunder.

—❧—

It was all Scott could do to keep from tearing off the man's head then and there. He'd seen the man skulking about the main lobby, looking suspicious, and even speaking to the front desk clerk for a few moments. Though he had his duties to tend to, he'd followed the man he now knew as Charlie Jarman down the east wing of the hotel. Scott had ducked out of view when Charlie paused to speak to a guest in one of the rooms, then he resumed tailing him all the way to the back of the hotel. If it hadn't been for the wedding planner stopping him to ask about private carriages for certain guests, Scott might have been able to intervene sooner.

Only momentarily stunned, Charlie recovered and hurled himself at Scott. "How dare you!"

With a strength gained from working with horses, Scott deflected Charlie's blow and swung at the man's jaw. But he connected with air. Before he realized where the quick-footed rat had gone, a fist shot up, smashing squarely into the ridge of bone over Scott's eye. White light flashed, and Scott blinked. His vision cleared just as Charlie came at him again. Scott blocked the jab and shoved Charlie away, backing the man a couple of steps beyond reach.

"I thought you two were more than just a hired man and his employer," Jarman huffed, his feet moving like a dancer. "Now I know Alyssa isn't quite the lady she claims to be. I'm just sorry I didn't get to her first."

Raging like a bull, Scott charged and swung, but once again, his adversary dodged him. "Stand still, you coward," he demanded. "This is a fight, not a jig."

"And this is boxing, you idiot."

Blood pounding in his temples, Scott plowed into the man, and, once again, Jarman danced away, but not before delivering a stabbing kidney punch. "You'll not lay a hand on me, or I'll—"

Ignoring what felt like a steel blade twisting in his back, Scott spun on the man with a powerful hook, proving him wrong. The impact practically lifted Jarman off the ground, and he descended in a crumpled heap. Walking over to the fallen man, his chest heaving, Scott looked down at him and seethed. "You stay away from

Alyssa and away from this hotel. If I see you again, I'm calling the authorities."

"I . . . I think you've broken my jaw," Jarman slurred as he pulled himself up using the post.

"It could have been your neck," Scott replied without sympathy. "And it *will* be your neck if you even hint Alyssa is anything less than a lady. Do I make myself clear?" he called after Jarman, who staggered toward the west side of the hotel without so much as looking back.

"Very," he managed. "But you'll pay for this," he muttered as he stumbled away, holding the side of his face.

Scott watched the good-for-nothing jerk until he disappeared. Every muscle in his body coiled like his fists, holding back the murderous rage still rampaging through his veins. Had Jarman not given up when he did—

Scott doubled over at the waist and pressed his fists into his sides, taking in huge gulps of air to calm himself. His body trembled as it unwound, and the pain that his fury had overridden now made itself known. Yet, even as his brain acknowledged it, soft sobs from a few feet away beat it back into submission. Alyssa!

He rushed to where she huddled against the carriage house wall, her body shaking with her strangled sobs. Kneeling in the dirt beside her, he laid a hand on her arm.

"Alyssa, sweetheart."

She answered him with what sounded like a combination between a hiccough and a gasp, making him wonder if he'd overstepped his bounds.

"He's gone."

Lifting her head, Alyssa sniffled but kept her eyes downcast.

"You're safe now."

"It was my f . . . fault," she murmured brokenly. "I . . . I shouldn't have been out here alone—"

"Nonsense," Scott objected. "He was nothing but a perverted slimeball. With a man like him, it's never your fault," he said softly, stroking away a cinnamon strand of hair from her face. "Don't even think it."

After wiping her cheeks and eyes, Alyssa raised her gaze to his. Her eyes widened. "You're bleeding!"

Surprised, he reached up to touch the tender spot near his eye.

"No! Don't touch it. It could become infected." As though she drew strength from his injuries, Alyssa hurried to her feet and grabbed his arm, practically dragging him through the back door to the carriage house. She jerked her head to the left and right, looking for something, then guided him over to a work table. There, she rummaged through an odd assortment of supplies and selected the ones she wanted.

Scott watched in disbelief. She was going to tend to his wounds with the same bandages and ointments the staff used on the carriage horses. And he was going to let her. But how did she know this stuff was even available?

Finally focused on tending to him, she didn't even pause to make eye contact before beginning her ministrations. With ointment on a cloth, she raised it to his temple.

"You don't have to do this," he mumbled half-heartedly. "I can take care of it myself."

"No!" she said a little too fast. "P-p-please. I m-m-must do this. I at least owe you this much."

The pleading in her eyes and tremble in her voice convinced him to agree. But it was more than that. Her eyes were saying "stay away," while her touch was saying "thank you" and "don't go." The compelling contrast fascinated him.

Scott remained still as she cleaned the cut at his temple. With Alyssa in such close proximity, an acute awareness overcame him. The faint scent of lavender mixed with the scent of horseflesh and ointment was an odd, but heady sensation, enough to make him think things he had no right—

"I want to thank you." Alyssa's soft words yanked him away from his unsettling thoughts, but then she hesitated. After a moment, she spoke again as she folded the bandage to place over the cut. She focused on her task and avoided his eyes. "If you hadn't arrived when you did, I—" Her words caught in her throat. "I can't bear to think what Charlie would have done."

A shudder overtook her, leaving her trembling in its wake. Every fiber in him wanted to pull her into his arms and hold her, stilling her fear. But after what she'd just endured, a man's arms were likely the last place she wanted to be. He clenched his fists and forced his arms to remain at his side as he watched a range of emotions cross her face. Gratefulness, panic, trepidation, agitation, and finally, control. When she moved to clean the cut at the corner of his mouth, he nearly lost his own restraint. Surely his teeth would crack if he clenched his jaw any tighter.

What he wouldn't give to know what Alyssa was thinking right now. If she was half as aware of him as she was of her, she definitely had better control than he.

Suddenly, her fingers grazed his lips. He inhaled a sharp breath. She froze.

Her touch unnerved him, and at the same time it awakened his senses. He placed his left hand over hers. It shook as he raised it to his mouth, but she did not resist. At its contact, liquid fire surged through his veins.

"Alyssa." The guttural quality of his voice surprised him. Her widened eyes suggested she, too, was shocked, and he wanted to take it back. But when those hazel pools met his, her expression softened and a soulful light shone from their depths. With his other hand, he cupped her cheek. Alyssa inhaled a tremulous breath, her lips parting. A lump formed in Scott's throat the size of his fist.

Slowly, he lowered her hand from his mouth and leaned forward. Her eyelids fluttered closed and her hand tensed, but she didn't try to remove it from his. All he could think about was what it would be like to kiss her and taste her lips. But before his mouth found hers, Ben's words invaded his thoughts.

The little gal's got a heap of hurt or something weighing down on her, and you're the first guy she's let get close since whatever happened to her happened.

Someone might as well have dumped a bucket of cold water over his head. How could he even think of taking advantage of her vulnerable state? With a jerk, he moved away and dropped her hand.

Alyssa stared, confusion and hurt clouding her eyes.

"I-I can't," he stammered. "It's too soon."

Her crestfallen face was nearly his undoing. He almost closed the gap between them and picked up where he'd left off. But it wouldn't be right. He'd pay the consequences of his actions, and so would she.

With a groan born of frustration, Scott instead grabbed her hand again and barreled back outside. "Come on," he said as he half-dragged her through the employee entrance at the back of the hotel.

Without a word, he meandered past carts and surprised wait staff and other essential hotel personnel until he reached the guest elevator. Punching the call button, Scott tapped his foot and watched the numbers light up as the elevator drew closer. He had to do this. Had to stay focused. Otherwise, he might cause irreparable harm to the childlike trust Alyssa had in him right now.

Finally, the ding signaled the car's arrival, and as soon as the doors opened, Scott stepped inside, pulled Alyssa in behind him, and immediately punched the number for her floor. He prayed someone else would join them, so he wouldn't have to endure the awkward silence as the elevator rose to the selected destination. But the doors closed without any other guests.

Halfway to the second floor, Alyssa sniffed. "Was it me?" her small voice asked. "Did I do something wrong?"

Scott closed his eyes. How in the world was he going to explain this to her? He just wanted to get her to Libby and put some distance between them. But if he said it out loud, the words might come out harsher than he intended. Still, he had to say something.

"No. It isn't you at all." He almost said it was him, but it would sound too much like a line. And the last thing he wanted her thinking is he wasn't sincere. So, why not the truth? Or at least part of it. Scott glanced down and noticed he hadn't released her hand, so he gave it a squeeze, trying to reassure her. "But if I had stayed another moment with you down there, I might've done something I'd regret."

Her sharp intake of breath said it all.

"I just need to know you're safe for now."

A second ding signaled their destination, and as soon as the doors opened, Alyssa stepped with him into the hall and headed down the hall to her room. He tapped twice on the door.

Come on, Libby, please be there.

He'd seen Libby head inside around lunchtime, but for all he knew, she could have gone off on another adventure to sample more of the amenities the hotel had to offer. But a moment later, the lock clicked and the door swung open. Libby's gaze went from Scott to Alyssa and back to Scott again, her eyebrows furrowing as she no doubt took note of the tear tracks on Alyssa's cheeks.

"What's going on?" Libby asked.

Scott took a deep breath and risked wrapping his arm around Alyssa's waist. The two ladies had to see he didn't intend any harm. "Libby, I hate to be the one to say this, but Alyssa had a run-in with some guy named Charles Jarman behind the hotel, and the man was well on his way toward acting out less-than-honest intentions when I put a stop to it."

Libby's jaw dropped, and her brows formed perfect arches. She looked to Alyssa—and so did Scott—in time to see Alyssa nod once, confirming his story.

"She's probably in shock," he said, "and could use a friend right now. Maybe even a hot shower."

"You got it," Libby replied.

After opening the door wider and propping it with her foot, Libby reached out, and Scott nudged Alyssa through the doorway to their suite. His arm slid from her waist, but he reached for her hand again and gave it a squeeze.

"Thank you," she whispered over her shoulder as the door swung closed.

Scott stood there staring at the room number on the door. Well, he'd made it. Barely. He scrubbed his hand across his mouth and chin. Thank God, Libby had been there, or he might've had to deal with his emotions and Alyssa's at the same time. It had disaster written all over it.

The responsibility he'd felt since he and Ben had talked was almost unbearable. And from the wounded look Alyssa had given him moments ago, it was nearly impossible to remain impartial. He just couldn't give in to his desires. Not yet. Not without knowing the truth behind her pain and who this Charlie guy was. Never mind all of her nonverbal cues told him she'd welcome his attention and his touch. His blood boiled at the thought.

But Libby had her now, and she'd take good care of Alyssa until he could gather his thoughts. Or at least until he could take a cold dip in the pool. And while it would cool him off, it wouldn't change his strong attraction to Alyssa or clear his mind of the hurt on her face. His was a no-win situation.

10

Alyssa crumpled in a heap and sank into the luxurious carpet as soon as she and Libby reached the inner sanctum of their suite. Libby brushed against her as she kneeled, and her arms came around Alyssa's shoulders as her friend leaned in close.

How could all of this have happened? Almost fourteen years had passed. She should have been safe enough to return by now. To finally do some healing. And what happens? She gets attacked by the same man who drove her away in the first place. Plus, Scott came to her rescue, and now Libby knew about the attack as well. Too many people, and too many questions, none of which she had the strength to answer right now.

"You go right on ahead and cry," Libby said. "When you're ready to talk, I'm here."

Alyssa pulled her knees up to her chest and dropped her head onto her folded arms. The tears fell like raindrops on a window, leaving tracks on her cheeks and soaking into the soft cotton of her sundress. Every second of the confrontation replayed itself in agonizing clarity. Alyssa could still feel Charlie's hands squeezing her arms, see the evil intent in his eyes, feel his breath on her face, smell his cheap cologne, and hear the menace in his voice. She shivered. Oh, if only Scott's rescue and sound beating had put an end to it all. But Charlie was still on the island. And she still had another week of vacation. How was she going to avoid Charlie and a possible repeat performance?

Better yet, how was she going to explain all of this to Scott? He said he needed to put some distance between them so he wouldn't do something he'd regret, but he'd be back. Would she be ready to face him, though? Especially after what she did once his cuts were cleaned. She might as well have come right out and told him to kiss her. She'd never in her life acted like this.

How had she managed to let things go so far? The attraction. The awareness. The desire. If Scott hadn't walked away, she wouldn't have been able to stop him. But fortunately, he *did* walk away. Two advances in one day were more than enough . . . even if one wasn't entirely unwanted.

"Ok," Libby stated. "I just can't take it anymore." She withdrew her arm, and Alyssa looked up as Libby did a little hop on her knees so she now faced Alyssa. "Please tell me what happened." She tucked a strand of hair behind Alyssa's ear. "You'll feel a lot better if you get it all out."

"You're right." Alyssa reached up and wiped the tears from her cheeks. From somewhere, Libby produced a Kleenex box, and Alyssa used several tissues to mop up the wetness around her eyes. Scrunching the tissues in her hand, she sniffled and stared straight ahead. "But will you be mad at me once I tell you?"

"Lys, you're my best friend. Through the good and the bad." She gave her a playful punch on the arm. "And it means you're stuck with me, no matter what."

In spite of the emotional battle taking place in her mind, Alyssa responded with a half-smile.

"Besides," Libby continued. "What kind of friend would I be if I up and ditched you or turned my back on you the moment you had a crisis or a dirty secret to share?" She placed a hand on Alyssa's arm. "I didn't desert you when your dad and granddad died or when you lost your first job because of malicious gossip from a jealous co-worker. I'm not going to desert you now." She gave Alyssa a little nudge. "Now, come on. Spill it."

"It will probably help if I start at the beginning," Alyssa said.

"You mean there's more to this story than just what happened today?"

Alyssa nodded. "And it's all connected."

"Go on."

"Do you remember the summer after my dad died, and I came back from this island with a completely different view of life?"

"How could I forget?" Libby shifted from her knees to sitting Indian-style. "You were like a zombie, walking around without showing much emotion, refusing to participate in anything not academically based, and rejecting every single guy who asked you out, no matter how drop-dead gorgeous he was."

Alyssa rolled her eyes. As if being gorgeous was the only thing of importance where men were concerned. Then again, to Libby, it tended to be the first checkpoint on her list. Well, Charlie was a good-looking guy . . . when he wasn't sneering or attempting to force someone to do what he wanted.

"Yeah, well, being gorgeous doesn't mean a thing when it comes to the type of man a guy is." Alyssa closed her eyes and took a deep breath. "I found it out that summer, and Charlie is the one who taught me the lesson."

Libby's jaw dropped. "The same Charlie who just attacked you downstairs?"

"Yes."

"You mean he's been holed up here on this island just waiting for you to return so he could finish the job?"

Alyssa winced. Lib was usually good at getting to the point, but did she have to put it so blatantly?

"Oh, sorry, Lys," Libby said, touching Alyssa's arm for a brief second. "It wasn't very thoughtful of me."

"No, you're right. And it appears Charlie has been waiting to some extent." She took a deep breath again. "Only he had no idea I had returned, at least not initially. He told me he'd heard some rumors somewhere and had to come find out for himself."

"So, what happened all those years ago to make it impossible for him to forget?" Libby gestured toward Alyssa. "And for you, too?"

The tears formed again and threatened to fall. Alyssa took the crumpled tissues and touched them to the corners of her eyes. She wasn't ready for this. The pain was too fresh.

"Lys, it's me, remember?" Libby chucked her under the chin. "You can do this. And you'll never be able to move on if you don't."

"But I've held it inside for so long, I'm not sure how to let it out."

"All the more reason to finally let go."

Alyssa glanced up at a restored antique dresser with its polished drawer handles and gleaming surface. The piece of furniture had stood the test of time. It had likely been used and abused, lovingly cared for, and restored to its former glory, but only after the process of being stripped bare so its true beauty could shine. If only she could be like the dresser. And maybe she could. Maybe this was where it all started.

"All right." Alyssa swung herself around to face Libby and mirrored her friend's position, then draped her arms on her knees. "I told you a lot about my visits to this island, but I don't believe I ever told you about Charlie."

Libby narrowed her eyes and pressed her lips into a thin line. "No, I would have remembered if you'd told me about a guy."

"Well, he and I stumbled upon each other one day down at the beach, and he seemed nice enough, so we started talking. When I introduced him to my dad and grandmother, Grandma told me we actually were distantly related—her grandmother and Charlie's grandmother's grandfather were brother and sister."

"Wow! How in the world had your grandmother been able to keep track for so long?"

Alyssa shrugged. "Maybe she has a detailed family tree some-where. I don't know. But when Charlie and I discovered we were distant cousins, we started hanging out all the time as friends. Each year got better and better. We had a great time while I was here, and then we'd say good-bye at the end of summer, and we'd both go our separate ways. Until the year after dad passed away. Then Charlie turned ugly."

"What happened to change him so much?" Libby wanted to know.

"I think he had some sort of fallout with his father. The man wasn't around much, and when he was, Charlie never had a kind word to say about him. One day, Charlie mentioned his mother had left them, and I sensed something had changed in him. But at first, he acted the same as usual. We went swimming, took bike rides around the island, had lemonade with Grandma, and did everything we'd done in the past. Then one evening Charlie and I were on the beach, and he asked me if I was going to keep coming every summer even though I could no longer come with my father."

Libby's eyebrows dipped low. "I don't understand. You were already there without your dad. Didn't it already prove you would?"

"I thought so. But then Charlie said something I still don't get, even this many years later."

"What?"

Alyssa tapped her fingers together and chewed on her lower lip. "He said I was old enough to make my own decisions, and I was free of my chaperone, so we could have a bit more fun." She opened her hands, palm up. "I can only assume he meant Dad, since we always came together, and a lot of what I did on the island had to be approved by Dad or Grandma first."

"So, then your chaperone wasn't gone," Libby pointed out. "Your grandmother was still here."

Alyssa tilted her head to the right. "You'd think so, wouldn't you? But maybe he felt Grandma was too old to keep up, and to him it meant time for more fun." She swallowed the bile in her throat. "Only I soon found out his meaning of 'fun' didn't match mine. When I pushed him away the first time, he laughed it off. But, when he tried again, and I refused to 'play' along," she said, making quote marks in the air. "He got forceful and overpowered me."

Libby reached out and took Alyssa's hands in her own. "Oh, Lys, I'm so sorry."

The warmth and pressure of tears came unbidden again. She sniffed and blinked several times. She had to get through this. With another deep breath, she plunged forward. "I fought him off as much as I could, but he managed to keep me pinned against the sand as he proceeded to show me his version of fun. I must have gotten a surge of adrenaline, and I was able to bring one of my knees up to his gut. He rolled off of me, and I made my escape, but by then it was too late," she finished in a whisper.

"No wonder you went home from here and started acting the way you did." Libby squeezed her hands. "I probably would have done the same thing."

"Today, Charlie said he wanted to take a walk to finish the conversation where we'd left off."

"Oh, the creep!" Libby crushed Alyssa's hands in her fists.

"Ow!" Alyssa tugged her hands free and rubbed them.

"Sorry." Libby gave her a sheepish grin. "I just can't believe the gall the jerk has, saying something like that to you."

"And if Scott hadn't arrived when he did . . ." Alyssa shuddered.

Libby covered one of Alyssa's hands with her own. "But he did. And it means Someone upstairs was watching out for you. Not once, but twice. Potential crisis averted." She narrowed her eyes. "Except . . ."

Alyssa tilted her chin to the right a little and peered closely at her friend. "Except what?"

"The way Scott looked at you when he brought you up here to our room, and the way you looked at him just before the door closed."

"What about it?"

Libby rested her fingers against her chin and tapped her upper lip. "I don't know yet. I can't put my finger on it. But I know something else happened. Something between the two of you."

Alyssa turned her head to the right and reached up to scratch near her eyebrow. She prayed Libby wouldn't be able to see the truth in her eyes. Her friend had a knack for ferreting out the truth, usually without too much effort. But this? These feelings Scott stirred inside of her? They were all too new, too fresh. She didn't even know if she could put them into words.

"You know you'd better finish the story before I run after Scott and bring him back to fill in the details."

"No!" Alyssa replied a little too quickly.

"Ah-ha!" Libby wagged her finger at Alyssa. "I knew it." A grin of triumph appeared on her face. "You've got a thing for him, don't you? Admit it."

Alyssa opened her mouth to refute it, but a knock at the door silenced her reply. She hopped up, eager to avoid the coming interrogation.

"Don't think you can get out of this so easily, Lys," Libby called to her back. "I will find out."

Alyssa opened the door and inhaled a sharp breath. "Grandma!"

Grandma took two steps into the suite, turned toward Alyssa, touched her hair, then pulled her into her arms. "Oh, child, come here."

With her head buried against her grandmother's shoulder, Alyssa let loose a fresh wave of tears and wept into Grandma's soft knit blouse. But a minute later, she raised her head and wiped at her eyes. "How did you know to come?"

Grandma gave her a half-smile. "Scott," she said simply. "He phoned and told me what had happened and said he would have a carriage at my house immediately to bring me to you."

Alyssa smiled through her tears. "You mean you rode with someone other than Scott as the driver?"

"Yes, dear. I did." Grandma cradled Alyssa's face in her wrinkled hands. "I might be set in my ways, but when it comes to family needing me, I can make an exception."

"Well, I'm so glad you're here," Alyssa said and stepped back. "And I'm all right." Well, maybe not all right, but definitely better than when she'd entered the room. "Or, at least I'm getting there," she amended, looking at her best friend. "Libby and I have been having a long overdue talk."

"Right," Libby chimed in. "Seems there's been a few important things Alyssa neglected to tell me about this Charlie fellow. Some things going way back to the last time she was here on the island."

Grandma snapped her gaze to Alyssa. "Scott told me it was Charlie who accosted you. But what's this about there being more to the story?"

Together, Alyssa and Libby filled in the blanks. When they finished, Grandma shook her head.

She pursed her lips. "I can't believe Charlie would do such a thing."

Libby crossed her arms. "Well, I think Scott did a pretty good job of setting him straight, Mrs. Denham." She angled a mischievous grin at Alyssa. "In fact, we were just discussing Scott when you knocked. I told Lys she must have feelings for him and was trying to get her to admit it, but she's acting like nothing happened."

Alyssa leveled a glare at her best friend, but Libby wouldn't be dissuaded.

"Come now, Libby." Grandma maintained a level tone to her voice. "Let's not take things too far."

Ah, good. A voice of reason. At least she had Grandma on her side.

"After all," Grandma continued, turning back toward Alyssa with a gleam in her eyes. "If we're not careful, our dear Alyssa might bottle up her feelings again. And if it happens, it might be another fourteen years before we find out anything more."

Libby's entire demeanor changed from a mischievous friend seeking a little gossip to a sleuth on a mission. This couldn't be good.

"You're absolutely right, Mrs. Denham," Libby replied. "We need to be careful and coax the information out of her."

All right. Enough of this dancing around. Alyssa took another step backward and smacked the surface of the dresser.

"It's not how it went at all. You're turning a minor exchange into something of extraordinary proportions."

"But of course!" Libby spread her arms wide. "It's what I do best! How else am I going to get out of you what I want?"

"And you know I have a way of coercing people to my way of thinking when I want something," Grandma chimed in.

Alyssa looked back and forth between Grandma and Libby. They couldn't be serious. Sure, they'd be curious. It was only natural. But this teaming-up thing? All to get some details Alyssa wasn't even sure she knew yet? Then, the corner of Libby's mouth twitched.

"Ah-ha!" Alyssa pointed a finger at each one in turn, mirth bubbling up from inside. "I knew it. You two couldn't fool anyone with your ruse."

Grandma placed one hand on her chest and faked an innocent expression. "Why, whatever do you mean?" Batting her eyelashes only made it worse.

Alyssa pressed her lips tight to hold back the laughter, and it came out more like a loud snort before bursting forth from her mouth. Their antics were just too much. But she needed this distraction.

The three of them leaned toward one another as merriment overtook them. Grandma recovered first, straightening and taking several deep breaths to regain her composure. Libby as well, her arms holding her middle as she gasped for air. Alyssa struggled to catch her breath. Her sides hadn't hurt as much in months. Not since she'd lost control of the box of tinsel icicles as they pulled down Christmas decorations from the attic, and the silvery threads dumped all over Libby.

"All right. All right." Grandma bounced her hands, palms down, as if attempting to quiet a rowdy group of children. "Let's make an attempt at being civil, shall we?"

Leave it to Grandma to get everything back under control. Always the voice of reason. She led by example as she padded across the carpet to one of three chairs near the double doors to the patio. Grandma chose first, and Libby and Alyssa followed suit. When they all settled into their respective seats, Grandma inhaled then released a single breath.

"Now, Alyssa . . . dear," she stated, placing emphasis on the last word as she folded her hands in her lap. "Why don't you finish your story about Scott before our curiosity gets the better of us?"

Alyssa couldn't escape this one. Grandma and Libby wanted to know everything, and though she didn't have much to tell at this point, she might as well share what she knew and felt. She crossed her ankles and adjusted the skirt of her sundress. Looking straight ahead, she delivered the answer she hoped they wanted to hear.

"It's not as big of a deal as you two are making it sound." At Libby's expulsion of breath, Alyssa rushed to continue. "Yes, Scott and I have spent some time together, and I'll admit I enjoy his company. But nothing else has happened," she said with a brief pointed look at Libby, who ducked her head. "After Charlie ran off, I helped treat Scott's wounds, and when I was done, he brought me upstairs to Libby, saying he needed some space. I think the fight with Charlie got him worked up a bit." She wasn't about to reveal the rest of what Scott said. It would get Libby going for sure.

"So, would you consider it an indication of his feelings?" Grandma asked. "Or are you still playing guessing games with each other?"

"I don't know." Moisture formed on Alyssa's palms, so she placed them on her thighs and slid them toward her knees. "There wasn't much time to talk after the altercation. But it's not as if he won't be around again soon. We still have the rest of those quilt blocks to collect, and he's promised to take us." She slid her gaze again to Libby. "Unless of course, someone happens to get him here before then to get *him* to talk."

Grandma gasped. "We would never do that!"

"Oh, I would!" Libby piped up. "Anything to get this girl back in the game."

Alyssa shrugged. "I hate to disappoint you both, but there just isn't anything else to say." Actually, there was, but sharing about the intense, wordless exchange she and Scott shared might not be the best thing to do right now.

"So, will you both be joining me for church on Sunday?" Grandma asked.

Well, that question came out of the blue. But at least they weren't on the topic of Scott anymore. "Of course," Alyssa replied. "I figured it was understood. Do you still go to the Little Stone Church down the road?"

"Yes. Reverend Carroll gives a fine sermon."

"Oh, and Libby, you're going to love the stained-glass windows." Alyssa flapped her hands and bounced in her seat. "There's one of Astor's agent for the American Fur Trading Company, and one of William Ferry, a missionary who set up a school for Indian children on the island and even shared the gospel message with them.

Each one of the windows in the church depicts some historic event in this area for the past one hundred years."

"Sounds fascinating," Libby replied then grinned. "I guess I should bring my camera."

"Definitely," Grandma said. "And maybe we can get a picture of all of us in front of the church." She looked at Alyssa. "You might even convince Scott and the other fellow you mentioned. Ben? Invite them to join us."

The teasing glint returned to Libby's face again. "Yes. Ben." She jutted her chin into the air an inch or two. "I can take care of him. And we can leave Scott to Alyssa." She smiled. "I'm sure there won't be any argument, especially since I know there is still more we're not being told. We'll discover it all eventually. And when we do . . ." A devilish gleam entered her eyes, and she rubbed her hands together like the mischievous soul Alyssa knew her to be.

"If the time comes when there's more to say," Alyssa said, "I promise you'll be the first to know."

"We'd better be!" Libby threatened.

In the meantime, Alyssa prayed she could maintain her focus, as well as keep a tighter rein on her emotions when she saw Scott again. Otherwise, she might do something *she'd* regret.

11

Aw, man, I wish I had been there!" Ben flipped up the first page on his itinerary clipboard and made a few notations on the paper.

Scott chuckled and ran his hand across the backs of one of the horses hitched to the carriage in front of the hotel. "I'm not sure Charlie would still be walking."

"Yeah, good point." Ben looked up from his work, one corner of his lip curled and fire in his eyes. Scott recognized the look. He had it yesterday when he happened upon the scene behind the hotel. "It just ain't cool, doing what you say the guy did," Ben continued. "He is lucky I wasn't there, or he would've been in much worse shape when I got through with him."

"Like needing an ambulance." And with Ben's years playing organized sports, plus all his time spent outdoors on the recreational activities with the hotel, it wouldn't have been a pretty sight.

"At least!" Ben replied.

Scott bent low to check the tires on the covered carriage. The gauge made a hissing sound and displayed the air pressure on the digital readout. It needed some air. The carriage had just dropped off a group from the recent ferry, and it was about to make a return trip for some guests coming in on a private yacht. Scott glanced up at his friend. "Good thing you weren't there, then. 'Cause I'm sure this Charlie fellow is going to file a complaint." He grimaced. "Or maybe even a harassment charge against me."

Ben slammed his palm down on the clipboard. "But you were defending a lady's honor!"

"For a guy like Charlie, it doesn't matter." Scott sighed. "At least, he was able to walk away." Though if Alyssa hadn't been there, Scott wouldn't have stopped at the jaw.

"You're a better man than me." Ben pressed the clipboard against the railing of the front hotel steps and leaned his weight against it. "If this jerk does report you, you know I've got your back."

"Thanks." Alyssa would no doubt vouch for him as well, if she would even be able to face Charlie again after what had happened. And if not, there was always Miss Edith and several other employees. Scott moved to the rear set of tires and set the gauge against the air spout.

Ben moved with him and leaned against the carriage. "Now, the real question is our little damsel in distress." He crossed one ankle over the other. "I wonder what she's thinking about you right now."

"I don't know. When I left her with Libby, I went and called her grandmother to let her know." He looked up at Ben and his crossed arms and gave him a wry grin. "And then I went for a swim."

"Yeah, I can imagine!" Ben let loose a low whistle. "Dude, I still can't believe you didn't at least kiss her after all of it."

Scott rested his forearm on one knee. "What, and do to her what I'd just kept that jerk from doing? No way."

Ben nodded. "Oh, yeah. Hadn't thought about it that way." He shifted and draped one arm along the side openings of the carriage. "Well, did you at least leave things on a good note? You didn't just dump her with Libby and run off, did you?"

"Not exactly." Scott went back to his task. "I told her I didn't want to do anything I might regret. She smiled at me and said 'thank you' before the door closed between us."

"Well, it's something." Ben nudged Scott with the toe of his sandal. "Now, what are you going to do? You got a plan or anything?"

"Nope." Scott shrugged. "Figured I'd give it a day and lay low. Then, I'd join them for church tomorrow and take it from there."

"You mean at the little church down the road?"

"Yep. Wanna come?"

The muscles in Ben's neck popped a bit. "I don't know. I have to work in the afternoon. Might want to sleep in."

"Libby will be there," Scott said with a grin. "And you can stand by to watch me botch things up with Alyssa, too."

Ben bent down and punched Scott in the arm. "Or bail you out if things start going south," he added.

"That too." Scott stood, ready to move around the carriage to the other side. "So you're coming?"

"You sure lightning ain't gonna strike me or something when I step inside the church? You know, it's been years since I've darkened the door of one."

"About time you did something about it, don't you think?" His friend looked like he needed just a little more nudging. "Come on. What's it going to hurt? It's just a little over an hour, and you'll be done." He winked. "And you'll make a good impression on the ladies, too."

Ben grinned. "Alright, I guess it won't cramp my style too much to go."

"Great." Scott returned the punch to the arm. "Service starts at ten-thirty. Don't be late."

"I won't."

Scott nodded toward the front porch. "Looks like your group for those parasailing lessons is here. Better get a move on."

Ben reached for his clipboard and shoved away from the carriage. "Yep." He took a step toward the stairs then stopped and glanced at Scott. "See you in the lounge tonight for the game?"

"Wouldn't miss it."

Scott walked around the carriage to finish the safety check. At least one good thing had come out of their conversation. Ben would be going to church. And if he could get his friend there, he might be able to talk to Alyssa without botching it too much . . . he hoped.

───❧❧❧───

Alyssa looked up from the little table by the French doors as the electronic lock on the door to her suite made its mechanical sound, and in walked Libby. She stuck a bookmark in the book she'd been reading and laid it on the table.

"Wow! What a swim." Libby toweled her hair dry as she padded across the floor toward Alyssa. "Not quite the same as the Olympic-sized pool at the fitness club back home, but refreshing all the same. Got in a great jog beforehand, too." She looked down at Alyssa. "If you hadn't chosen to stay holed up in this room, I'd have asked you to join me." She reached out and touched Alyssa's shoulder. "But I understand why you don't want to go out."

"Reading can be a fun activity, too," Alyssa replied, but she didn't sound too convincing, even to her own ears.

"As fun as getting a tooth pulled, maybe." Libby stuck out her tongue and wrinkled her nose. "No thank you."

"You should give it a try some time. You might like it."

"And give up all of my crazy activities? I might miss something." She paused. "Or someone," she added.

Alyssa shook her head. Right back at the never-ending line of men trailing in Libby's wake. "At least it gave me a few hours of peace and quiet." She sighed. "Haven't had much of it this week."

Libby gave her a knowing look. "Everything been quiet around here? No crank calls or unwelcome visitors?"

"Not a soul." Alyssa knew her friend was talking about Charlie and anything he might have done while Libby was out. "It's been me and my book and this amazing view of the lake the entire time."

"Good." Libby took a step back and plopped onto the edge of the nearest bed. "At least the creep hasn't been stupid enough to try anything today."

Alyssa grinned. "No, and if he had, I'm sure my watchdog would scare him off."

"Yep." Libby brought up her hands in clawlike fashion to either side of her face and made a growling noise while baring her teeth. "My bite is worse than my bark."

"You're not kidding." Alyssa threw back her head and laughed. "And anyone who dares cross you had better watch out for those vicious claws."

Libby winked. "Exactly!"

Alyssa sobered and swung around in her seat to face her best friend. "You know, Lib, I am so lucky to have you." There were times when she had no idea why Libby put up with her, but her life wouldn't be half what it was without Libby in it. "So many others have come and gone, and some have paid lip service only to desert me when things got a little rocky."

"Like I said a few days ago, Lys, you're stuck with me." She reached across the distance between them and grabbed Alyssa's hand. "Like it or not, with all of our zany quirks and habits, we're good for each other."

"A friend knows all about you and still loves you," Alyssa quoted from a plaque her mother had hanging in the hallway near the kitchen. She'd read it more times than could possibly be counted and often wondered what it would be like to have a friend like that. Now she knew.

"You got it, chica. I'd say we both fit the bill quite nicely ... even if I do say so myself." Libby released Alyssa's hand and slid back on the bed a bit, crisscrossing her legs. "Because it's not like I don't have my own haunts throwing a wrench in my plans from time to time. Everyone has them."

"No," Alyssa said, reaching out to caress the cover of her book. "But you haven't held onto them for a decade and a half, bottling up the emotions and fears and everything else to go with it. You—and it seems like everyone else—learn to deal with them." And blocking out the painful memories.

"True, but I just go about dealing with my pain in a different way." Libby closed her fists and brought them to her chest. "You hold everything inside, and I brush it off," she said, spreading her arms wide, "seeking out the next thrill to come along. Who's to say which one of us is right or wrong?"

"At least, you have fun while doing it."

"Are you saying you haven't had any fun in your life because of this awful experience hanging around your neck?" Libby stuck her fists on her hips. "Because if you do, I might just have to use your book to whack you upside the head." She moved her hands to grasp an imaginary book and swung it in Alyssa's direction.

Alyssa held up her hands, protecting herself from the pretend onslaught. "No, no! Don't hit me." She ducked and drew her legs up as close to her chest as she could. "I bruise easily."

"So, I've noticed," Libby replied with a somber nod at Alyssa's marked wrist. "Did that loser do this to you?"

Alyssa turned her wrist back and forth and looked at the purplish-blue coloring of her skin near the bone. "Yes," she said in a small voice. Nearly identical to the evidence Charlie had left the last time, only then she'd kept it covered up with long sleeves and wide-band bracelets. "The unfortunate side of having fair skin. Everything shows up, and there's no hiding a thing."

"Oh, I don't know. If he was as rough as you said he was all those years ago, you did a pretty good job then of keeping it a secret." Libby leaned back on her hands. "At least I never noticed anything. And if anyone would have noticed, if would have been me."

"Libby Duncan, with the amazing powers of insight and observation."

"Good at uncovering the truth when the time is right and jumping on it," she said with a mock pounce, her hands out in front of her on the bed.

Alyssa gave her friend a sheepish grin. "I guess I'm getting lax in my old age. Not doing as good a job at hiding the evidence."

"Or else," Libby said with a pointed glance, "you're realizing being a little more transparent is a good thing."

"Maybe." She let her legs fall back so her feet touched the floor, then stretched out with her arms above her head. "But it's going to take some getting used to, all this not bottling up feelings and actually working through the problems as they happen." Alyssa wasn't foolish enough to think this big issue was the last one she'd have. There'd be more. This one just ruled her life for far too many years. If only she'd let go of it sooner.

"It's why God gives us friends. It'll get easier with time, and you'll have me here to help." Libby placed her hands down on the bed in front of her, fingers facing each other as she leaned forward. "As long as you promise me one thing."

"What?"

She grinned. "You'll give me a good knock upside the head if you catch me running away and avoiding the commitment thing."

"Oh, you can count on it," Alyssa replied, letting one corner of her mouth turn up in a grin.

"Good" Libby glanced down at her watch. "Oh! What time were we supposed to meet your grandmother?"

"Umm, four o'clock, I believe," Alyssa answered. "Why?"

"Because it's a little after three now." She sprung off the bed and dashed toward the bathroom. "I still have to shower and change and grab an extra outfit for dinner tonight."

"You can always come back to the room and change once we return," Alyssa pointed out. It's what she'd planned to do. "No sense lugging an extra outfit with us to Grandma's if we don't have to."

Libby poked her head out of the bathroom. "Good point." She disappeared for a few seconds then reappeared. "And did your grandmother say why we were meeting her at her place? Because we aren't going on any more quilt block missions until Monday."

"No, she didn't."

"So, how do I know what I'm supposed to wear, then?"

Alyssa shrugged. "Just dress comfortably. I'm sure it'll be fine."

"Ok."

This time, the door closed shut with a click, and then Alyssa heard the water running. Honestly. She'd have thought someone had invited Libby to the governor's summer house or something, the way she fretted about her wardrobe. Alyssa glanced down at her embellished jeans and simple tunic top. Yep. Just fine. No reason to get all worked up over anything.

———◦◦◦◦———

"I'm glad to see you girls have dressed simply and comfortably," Grandma said as soon as they'd entered the cottage.

Alyssa nudged Libby. "Told you so."

Libby hitched her chin up a bit and didn't reply. "So, what are we doing, Mrs. Denham?"

Grandma walked around to the front of the sofa and uncovered a square wooden contraption with pins around the sides and pieces of cloth on it. "I'm going to teach you girls some basic quilting skills, and you're going to help me start assembling this quilt."

Libby expelled her breath, vibrating her lips. "Miss Dottie said it'd only be a matter of time before you suckered us into something like this."

"Dottie said so?" Grandma pursed her lips. "I might have to talk to her about spoiling my surprise."

"Grandma, this isn't so much a surprise as a form of punishment." Alyssa stepped over and rested her hands on the back of the sofa. Maybe if she kept a barrier between her and the project of doom, she could find a way to avoid it. "You know I can barely sew a button on a shirt, let alone attempt to make something into some semblance of a pattern."

"Yeah, and I'm with Lys," Libby added. "If I need something repaired or sewn, I take it to my mother. Or I pay someone else to do it."

"Because, my dears, there are a great many lessons to be learned from the simple act of quilting, and if nothing else, it will give the three of us a chance to visit more."

Libby inched closer, as if the wooden frame was going to jump up and bite her at any moment. "But we can visit in the comfort of the posh hotel up on the hill. Why throw work into the mix?"

"I've opened up my home to you, and you have traipsed about this island, visiting my friends and collecting pieces of this quilt all week. The least you can do is allow me to repay you by helping you learn a few basics. They'll go a long way toward helping you in many other areas of life." She smiled. "We'll call them essential life skills."

And there it was. The persuasive technique Grandma always used to bring others around to her way of thinking. Of course, this time, it wouldn't take as much persuasion on her part, as she had a captive audience. And Alyssa would never refuse her grandmother. Libby likely wouldn't either.

Alyssa sighed. "Where do we start?"

"It's two against one." Libby looked at Alyssa first, then at Grandma. "Guess I don't have much of a choice, do I?"

"No, you don't," Grandma replied. "So, come over here, and let's get moving. We don't have much time before dinner, and I want to at least lay out the pieces we have, so we can get ready for the individualized blocks."

"Might as well make the best of it, I guess," Libby said and moved to one side of the frame.

Alyssa stepped around the sofa and stood opposite Libby. "Show us what you need us to do."

Grandma gestured toward a large square of material laid out on the floor near the fireplace. "I've already established a background fabric, and from the blocks we've already collected, you've no doubt seen the basic pattern we'll be using."

"You mean those star shapes behind the images in the center?" Libby asked.

"Exactly."

Alyssa fingered the frame and glanced over it to the floor where the material lay. "So, what do we do now?"

Grandma retrieved the pieces from her desk against the wall. "Now, we're going to divide up the blocks and begin piecing everything together by hand."

By hand? Alyssa didn't know much about quilting, but hadn't sewing large things by hand gone out with the last century? "Don't you have a machine you can use for this sort of thing?"

"No, child," Grandma replied with a smile. "I haven't been able to part with my hard-earned money to invest in one. Besides, I enjoy the process by hand too much to let a machine do it for me. I'll leave all those new-fangled mechanical contraptions to you younger folks."

Libby moved around the quilt frame and stood to Grandma's right. "What's going to happen once we've got all the blocks sewn together?"

Grandma glanced over at Libby. "We'll lay the pattern onto the backing and batting and get it onto the frame. We'll need to sew together the layers for a secure finish, and it includes piecing together the top and basting it with batting and backing material. Afterward, we'll wrap it in archival paper and present it to the gift recipient."

Alyssa moved to Grandma's other side and reached down to touch what would become the back of the quilt. "You mean you're not keeping this one?" This was a surprise. Grandma had said she'd wanted to get this done for years. And now she was planning to give it away?

"No, dear. I'm assembling it for someone special."

"Who?" Alyssa and Libby asked simultaneously.

"You'll find out in due time. Now, are we ready to get started?"

12

Alyssa slid into the same row at the little church where her grandmother had sat every Sunday all the years she'd lived on the island. After fluffing the chiffon overlay of her floral-print dress, Alyssa smoothed her hands over the polished wood pew then reached for a hymnal from the back of the pew in front of her. They'd upgraded since she'd last visited. Flipping through the pages and landing on one she knew by heart, Alyssa smiled when her favorite hymn was still on the same page she'd remembered.

"I see you haven't forgotten your way around a hymnal, dear," Grandma whispered with a smile on her face.

"Of course not, Grandma. They still sing some hymns in the churches in Grand Rapids." She nudged her grandmother. "Even if it's all digital now and displayed on a screen at the front of the sanctuary."

Grandma smoothed her hands over her own hymnal and shook her head. "There is something about turning the pages of a book no screen or electronic gadget will ever replace."

"For the most part, I agree," Alyssa replied. "But I have to admit, I do enjoy my handheld tablet. It gives me just about everything I need at my fingertips and is portable, too."

"You keep your gadgets, dear," Grandma said, patting Alyssa's hand. "I'll stick with my old-fashioned books."

Someone from the pew behind them tapped Grandma on the shoulder. She turned away from Alyssa and chatted. Alyssa shifted her attention to the front of the room at the ornate rose window above the altar. Both sides curved to a point at the top and the circle in the middle glowed red-orange with a patterned mixture of blues in the center. The golden background behind the circle glowed with the illuminating sunlight.

Below the window sat the altar, with two Queen Anne chairs adorning either side of the pulpit on the elevated platform. So different from the stage at her own church, with ample room for the worship team, musicians, and even the choir on some select Sundays. And it didn't include the large screens at the front, alternating between a preservice slideshow of upcoming events and information, and the words to the songs they sang during each service. Did she like one more than the other?

A hush fell over those gathered as the soft piano and old organ both played the opening notes to the first hymn they'd sing. Everyone stood to join together in song. Alyssa turned to smile at Grandma, their melded voices reminding Alyssa of how many Sundays they'd spent together doing the same thing. Before the end of the second hymn, a rich baritone joined in just slightly off-key, and her heart skipped a beat. She turned to see Scott had slid in beside her on her left. A glance the other way, and there stood Ben on Libby's right.

"Close your mouth, child," Grandma leaned over and whispered. "You might catch more of those flies again."

Alyssa snapped her jaw shut. When had it fallen open? It wasn't much of a surprise to see Scott and Ben in church with them. Perhaps Ben more so than Scott, but certainly neither worthy of a gaping mouth. What would the men think of her if they saw her staring?

At the conclusion of the final hymn, everyone took their seats, and Reverend Carroll stood from one of the Queen Anne chairs to walk to his position behind the pulpit.

"A blessed day to be in the house of our Lord. Thank you all for coming to worship with us this morning." He opened his Bible to a designated spot then placed both hands on either side of the podium. "I'd like to begin today talking about forgiveness and move into the simplicity of faith, of trusting God with the big as well as the little things in our lives."

Alyssa had a difficult time focusing on the message with Scott sitting right next to her. They hadn't yet spoken about the events from Thursday evening, and now they were together in church. It could be worse. He could completely avoid her and everything she did for the remainder of her vacation. But he had chosen to come and share their pew. And he'd brought Ben with him. As a buffer or for support, she didn't know. Or maybe Ben had come on his own. Libby obviously didn't care. She sat there with a huge grin on her face as the Reverend presented the points of his talk. Alyssa wished she could do the same.

About midway through the sermon, Scott reached over and covered her hand with his own. She flinched, then winced, sure he was going to yank back his hand. But instead, he held firm. Alyssa glanced over at him, and at first, he stared straight ahead. Then, he looked down at her, and the corners of his mouth turned up just slightly in a soft smile. She returned the smile and tried to center her attention again on the sermon. Scott knew exactly what he was doing, and he was trying to tell her so. If only she could move past those walls she'd erected years ago. Maybe it was time to let someone else in close enough to help her chisel away at the barriers.

Scott placed a hand at the small of Alyssa's back and escorted her down the aisle toward the double doors to the right at the back of church. The gauzy part of her dress draped over the part underneath, giving it an ethereal quality, especially when the breeze from outside caught the material and sent it floating on the wind. She'd actually let him keep his hand covering hers for the latter part of the sermon. When she flinched, his instinct had been to immediately pull back his hand, but he didn't. He almost hadn't done anything for fear it was too soon. It looked like his boldness had paid off.

"Thank you for coming today." The Reverend greeted Libby and Scott first, shook their hands, and turned a warm smile on Miss Edith. "Another fine morning for worship, Edith. I'm glad to see you've brought some family and friends with you today."

Miss Edith returned the smile then turned to extend her arm toward Alyssa. "Yes, this is my granddaughter, Alyssa, and the other young lady is her best friend, Libby Duncan."

The Reverend peered at Alyssa and furrowed his brow. "A much younger Miss Denham the last time you were here, if I'm not mistaken."

Alyssa nodded and was impressed the man remembered. "Yes, Reverend. I've been away for a while, but I've finally come back to this island I love."

Miss Edith gestured toward Scott and Ben, palms up. "And these two gentlemen, you might know. Ben Webster and Scott Whitman both work at the Grand."

"Ah, yes." The Reverend nodded. "I believe Ben here was fortunate enough to give my youngest granddaughter lessons in waterskiing last summer."

Ben laughed, and his shoulders shook. "Oh yeah, I remember her, an adventurous little gal. She must have fallen into the water at least a dozen times or more, but she wouldn't give up." He winked at the Reverend. "Quite a lot of spunk in her."

"Indeed," the Reverend replied. "Takes after her father, a career Navy SEAL."

"Guess it's a good thing I let her keep at it until she mastered it, then." Ben whistled. "Wouldn't have wanted her father to come track me down later."

"True, true." The Reverend clapped Ben on the shoulder. "So, will I be seeing you next week then?"

"Maybe," Ben replied. "You just might."

"Well, you folks enjoy the rest of your Sunday."

Scott and Alyssa took their turns shaking the Reverend's hand before moving with Miss Edith, Ben, and Libby to the concrete patio at the front of the church.

"So, what did you think?" Scott asked Ben as soon as all five of them stood near the black wrought-iron fence about twenty feet from the main doors.

"I actually liked it," Ben replied. "He said a lot of good things. Stuff I never thought about before."

"Such as?" Miss Edith asked.

"Well, like how much faith I already have in the everyday things in my life and how easy it should be to trust God when I can so easily trust in all this other stuff." Ben shrugged. "Just hadn't ever seen or heard it put that way."

Libby sidled up to Ben, wrapping her arms around one of his and gazing up at him. "Well, I know I'm glad you came. Certainly made my morning immensely better."

"And I'm happy to see you've joined us as well," Miss Edith added. "I mentioned to the girls the other day I'd hoped to have a picture of all of us here at the church. It's where Alyssa's parents were married and where Alyssa herself was baptized. Plus, if I'm not mistaken," she said, leveling a glance at Ben. "This is now the first church you've been to in a number of years. Am I right?"

Ben winced. "Guilty."

Miss Edith waved off his remorse. "Never you mind, young man. There will be no condemnation here today. Or any day." She clapped her hands together. "Now, where would the best place be to snap a photo?" She looked around, eyeing each little crevice and secluded area.

"What about on the other side of this fence?" Alyssa suggested. "There's a beautiful group of trees there to provide some shade, and if we used the stone benches, we could get the church in behind us and maybe even some of these beautiful red geraniums planted in the bushes near the fence." She pointed just beyond the area. "We could even use the stone wall there to prop the camera for its timed delay."

Scott surveyed the spot Alyssa pointed out, then glanced back at the church. She had an excellent eye for color, placement, and optimal space to create just the right effect. He couldn't believe she kept herself chained to a desk in an office job. She sure was missing out on a fantastic opportunity to maximize her skills.

"Splendid." Miss Edith clapped her hands. "Yes, it will do nicely." She waved her hands in rapid motion, as if shooing chicks or hens into the pen. "Come, come. Let's get organized and take the picture. I've got dinner waiting in the crock pot at my cottage, and of course, you're all invited."

It took some shuffling, but they finally got themselves arranged. Alyssa stood at the wall to set up the camera. Scott made sure to carve out a place for her in front of him. With Miss Edith in the center and Libby and Ben to her left, it hadn't been difficult at all. He definitely wanted a copy of this one.

"Everybody ready?" Alyssa called. "Once I hit this button, we'll have ten seconds to get situated again." She touched her finger to the top of the camera. "And . . . go!"

After prancing back to the four of them, she quickly slipped into place and stood as they counted down the seconds. "Six, five, four, three, two, one."

A series of red-light blinks flashed faster and faster until they stopped.

"Is it done?" Ben asked through his frozen smile.

"I believe so," Alyssa replied. "It won't flash since we're outside." She stepped away from her spot. "But let's take another one just in case."

The procedure repeated itself, only this time, when Alyssa slid into place, Scott leaned down close to her ear. He swallowed once, sending up a silent prayer. This had to be done right.

"I'd like to invite you to join me on the porch this evening after dinner." He paused to let his words sink in. "Meet me around eight?"

The others counted down again, but Alyssa remained silent. Then, the slightest nod of her head signaled her agreement.

The blinking red light stopped, and it looked like the shutter closed then opened again. They had their special moment preserved for all time.

"Please, be careful," he continued as the group moved apart. The Charlie fellow was still skulking around the island somewhere. Alyssa didn't need a repeat of the incident from a few days ago. "Don't go off anywhere on your own, and make sure someone is with you at all times. I promise to be on the porch promptly at eight."

"Good, now let's go get some food," Ben was the first to say. "I'm starved!" He draped an arm across Libby's shoulders and led her toward their carriage.

Scott offered one arm to each of the ladies, and they followed behind. This evening couldn't come fast enough.

Alyssa stood, looking out across the lake to the west. Libby stood with her. Scott hung back near the wall of the hotel. Her simple yet elegant gown hugged her form in all the right places, and the evening breeze stirred the hem, flaring it out just a bit. The material caught the lights from the porch just right and shimmered as it moved.

Scott reached up and loosened his tie a bit, making it much easier to breathe. Or did the conversation he was about to have make his breath jam in the middle of his throat? No time like the present to find out. With a deep breath, he pushed away from the wall and came up behind the two ladies. Libby noticed him first and backed away. He mouthed the words *thank you* to her as she left the two of them alone.

"It's beautiful," Alyssa said, breaking the silence, and Scott didn't know if she was talking to him or to Libby. Did she realize he now stood with her and Libby didn't?

Scott followed the line of her gaze out from the porch and into the darkness to the left at the lighted Mackinac Bridge separating Lake Michigan from Lake Huron and then crossing the Straits of Mackinac to connect the main part of Michigan to the Upper Peninsula. He wasn't sure what to say, so he stepped up beside her and dropped a piece of trivia from one of his many rehearsed speeches.

"You know the bridge is five miles long."

"Yes," she said softly. "And it took three years to build it."

"Quite a big moment when it was finished. Michiganders could finally travel between both parts of the state by car instead of boat."

"Yes," she replied, her voice a bit melancholy. "But then they miss out on this beautiful island by not traveling via the water."

"Plenty of folks still come. Just look at how busy this hotel is during the summer months." If she wanted to talk tourism and island trivia, he would oblige. But he'd have to steer this conversation better if he wanted to get out what he came to say.

"I guess so."

"And it's still making a name for itself through the movies filmed here, as well as general word of mouth." He flattened his hands on the front railing of the porch. "Besides, if folks were missing out so much, do you think they'd be adding more rooms or shops to the Grand every year?"

"No, I guess not."

Scott inched just a little closer to Alyssa. "You already know about *Somewhere in Time* and probably about the suite they added a few years back, right?"

"The one dedicated to Jane Seymour?"

"Yes. Using furniture and linens she designed herself with the Grand in mind."

"I knew about the linens," she said, "but not the furniture. It's a suite I'd love to see."

Scott brushed his fingernails on his suit coat and inspected them. "We just might be able to arrange it while you're here."

Alyssa finally turned to look at him, her entire face lit up and a broad smile on her lips. "Oh, yes, how wonderful!"

"And speaking of movie-related dedications, did you know the hotel pool was named for Esther Williams and her comedy, *This Time for Keeps?* It was another one filmed on this island." He pressed his lips together and looked off to the right. "Back in 1947, I believe."

"Grandma talks about it a lot." Alyssa quirked one corner of her mouth and tapped her finger to it. "But you know, I don't think I've ever seen it. We usually end up watching *Somewhere in Time* instead."

Scott grinned. "Gee, I can't imagine why."

Alyssa ducked her head and tucked a strand of her wavy hair behind her left ear. The faintest hint of a blush appeared on her cheeks. Scott had tried so hard the past few days to dwell on something other than his attraction to her. Taking a dip in the pool, losing himself in tasks for his jobs, and even walking the perimeter of the island yesterday. None of it worked.

Sure, he'd stayed busy, but every time he had just a few minutes of downtime, Alyssa popped into his head. And not only her, but the replay of the scene in the carriage house behind the hotel. No matter what he did, he couldn't remove the memory of Alyssa's face inches from his own or the flash of desire he'd seen just before her eyelids drifted shut. She'd wanted his kiss as much as he'd wanted to give it. And now, here she stood, mere inches away, agreeing to meet with him alone.

Scott reached for Alyssa's hands and held them, gently turning her to face him. "Alyssa," he said, his voice guttural and raspy.

<hr />

Alyssa looked down at the hands covering hers, his tanned skin a stark contrast to her pale shade. She gave him a wary look. "Scott, please," she whispered. "I . . . I'm not sure I'm ready for this."

If truth be told, she *was*, but she wasn't sure if she wanted him to know it.

"And what does your gut tell you?" Scott asked, as if he'd read her thoughts. "Because I know sometimes the head can be at odds with the rest of the body. It's easy to get confused." He dipped his head low and compelled her to look at him. "Trust me."

"It's easier to trust when I know there's no cause for concern." She toyed with the idea of removing her hands from his, but it felt so good to have more than his verbal reassurance.

"And are you concerned about what I might do or what you might?"

She inhaled a sharp breath. "Why do you ask?"

Scott caressed the backs of her hands with his thumbs. His touch stirred a desire in her she didn't think was possible, but his nearness offered a great deal of comfort, too. He wouldn't try anything without her permission. She knew it.

"I noticed when I first approached you seemed nervous, a bit distracted, and you filled any uncomfortable silence with words."

Alyssa ducked her chin. "Oh." And she had hoped sticking to safe topics might cover up the inner turmoil. Obviously, it hadn't. Scott had seen right through her unsuccessful attempts. And now he wanted to know more.

He dropped one of her hands to touch his fingers to her chin and raise her head to again meet his gaze. "Hey," he said softly. "You can't be expected to have an answer for everything. Life isn't *that* perfect."

He moved his index finger back and forth on the underside of her chin. She quelled the shiver starting somewhere near the base of her spine. Instead, she got lost in the coffee-colored depths of his caring eyes.

As if he had read her mind, he jerked his hands back and put a few extra inches between them.

"Sorry." He averted his gaze for a brief second then released a short sigh. "So, we have a conversation to finish, don't we?"

Alyssa blinked a few times. Conversation? Oh, right. The one they didn't get to finish the other day because Scott had needed some space. She'd better get a handle on her emotions. And fast.

She wet her lips and swallowed. "I suppose."

A dimple in his right cheek appeared, accompanying his grin and raised eyebrow. "You suppose? You're not gonna make this easy on me, are you?"

She shrugged. "It's just I'm not sure I can do this. It's been a long time since . . ." She shuddered. "Since I've let anyone get this close."

"Especially a man," Scott pointed out, his voice holding no malice, no sense of an ulterior motive.

"Yes," she breathed, barely able to speak.

Scott took a step closer and resumed his previous hold on her hands. "Well, how about we start by you relaxing just a bit." He gave her hands a squeeze. "It's just me. And I'd never do a thing to hurt you."

"I know." Alyssa swallowed again. "But I still have to be careful."

His thumbs moved in their circular motion again, everywhere they touched leaving a trail of heat searing into her skin.

"Yes," he replied, his gaze earnest. "But I promise I won't give you any reason to worry at any time when you're with me."

Alyssa didn't trust her voice, so she nodded.

"We'll take it one step at a time. And the first step is telling me what history you have with this Charlie fellow."

She gasped. How did he know? Alyssa narrowed her eyes. "What makes you think we have a history?"

"Because even as beautiful as you are, I have a hard time believing a random guy would up and attack you like he did." Scott gave her fingers a little squeeze. "And there's the whole matter of you avoiding this island for all those years. Doesn't take Einstein to put two and two together."

There was no teasing, no condemnation. Just gentle encouragement and an honest desire to know the truth. How could she deny him?

Alyssa took a shuddering breath. "Okay. I'll tell you everything."

And she did. Everything about Charlie, how they met, her connection to him, all the way up until the fateful night on the beach. And through it all, Scott never said a word. When she got to the end, he tightened his grip until she winced.

"Oh, sweetheart, I'm sorry."

The endearment flowed so easily from his lips. Was he even aware he said it?

"Now I know why you act the way you do and why you're so skittish or uncertain around men." Scott reached up and caressed her cheek. "I'd say it's high time you learned we're not all out to get you." He gave her a teasing grin. "In fact, I'll even volunteer to do the teaching."

Alyssa stared long and hard, unable to break free from the pull of his gaze.

"Whatever it takes for you to fully trust me," he continued. "And no matter what happens, I will always be a friend."

Oh, how she wished he could become something more. He actually cared about her hesitation and knew the reason for it. And the softness in his eyes all but wore down her determination to maintain a safe distance from him emotionally. No. She dare not risk it. The threads of her resolve were thin enough as it was. If she didn't control her emotions, those threads would snap and she'd be pulled along under the safe surface to the tangled and chaotic layers below.

"For starters," Scott said, snapping Alyssa from her thoughts. "I'd like to kiss you. But not unless you agree."

Alyssa had no idea what to do. No man had ever asked for her permission before. Then again, the only guy she'd let get this close had been Charlie. So, she had no real basis for comparison. At least not with that. With Scott, it was different. Where Charlie wanted to take, Scott asked. Where Charlie had forced, Scott gently invited. And where Charlie focused only on himself, Scott made it all about her. Except for the restrained passion in his eyes. She'd seen it three days ago in the carriage house, too. And he'd managed to walk away, no matter how much they'd both wanted more. Yes, she could definitely trust him in this.

Alyssa moistened her lips once more. "I . . . I think I'd like that," she breathed.

With agonizing slowness and care, Scott took a step closer and reached up to cradle her face with his hands. Her mouth parted and her breath caught in her throat as his face drew nearer to hers. The seconds ticked in half-time with her pulse beating in her chest. His breath fanned across her cheeks, and his features blurred. Her eyes drifted shut, and she waited for the touch of his lips on hers.

Then, his mouth brushed hers with the airy lightness of the evening breeze, stirring and teasing, taunting. Every part of her wanted him to close the gap. She'd never wanted a man's touch so much. But it didn't come.

Alyssa opened her eyes to find Scott poised just an inch or two away. He grinned down at her, a self-conscious grin on his face.

"I had to be sure you were ready," he said with a wink.

Before she could respond, their lips met, and he paid homage to her mouth. Tender and forceful, reverent and defiant. A sweet mix of pure desire and respect. Everything about his kiss left her wanting more. All too soon, it ended, and he pulled back.

Alyssa opened her eyes, trying hard to hide the disappointment from him.

"And with this, Alyssa sweetheart, I *need* to say good night." He raised her hand to his lips and placed a kiss there, grinning over her knuckles. "Otherwise, I'm going to forget myself and ruin all the progress we've made tonight."

Scott beckoned to someone with his finger, and from somewhere on the porch Libby appeared. Her best friend wrapped an arm around her waist as Scott backed farther and farther away. One pivot on his heel and he was gone. But Libby was there.

"Come on, Lys dear," Libby said, urging Alyssa toward the lobby. "We've got some talking to do."

13

Alyssa paused in her stitching and raised a hand to cover her mouth as a yawn escaped. She shook her head and reached for the tall glass of Grandma's lemonade sitting on the end table, then took a sip. The sugary tartness with a hint of mint awakened her taste buds. This had to stop. She'd endured sleepless nights before, and they'd never worn her out this much.

"What's the matter, dear?" Grandma asked. "Aren't you feeling well this morning?"

"She didn't get much sleep, Mrs. Denham," Libby answered.

"I'm fine," Alyssa replied, scrunching her nose at her friend.

"Oh? Is something on your mind?" Grandma pushed the needle through the fabric in her hand and pulled it back through to the top. "Perhaps something you want to talk about?"

"No, more like someone," Libby said with a grin.

Alyssa sighed. She kind of wanted to keep all these new feelings to herself for a bit. Savor them, dwell on them, and maybe even figure out what she was going to do next.

Grandma continued stitching, glancing from the blocks she pieced together to Alyssa to Libby and back to the quilt sections. A smile played at the corner of her mouth. "Now, I'm intrigued."

No way would Alyssa get out of this one. Just like the interrogation Libby gave her last night. And she *did* promise both Libby and Grandma they'd be the first to know if anything developed with Scott or if she had anything to share. Maybe having some more girl talk wouldn't be a bad thing.

Alyssa looked over at Grandma and tried to imitate the way she assembled the blocks. It wasn't as easy as she'd thought.

"Be sure to stitch in a straight line, dear. And Libby, don't forget to tie off the end of the thread when you're finished with each seam." Grandma resumed her work. "Now, Alyssa, let's hear about this sleepless night you had."

"There isn't much to tell," Alyssa replied, keeping her attention focused on the quilt blocks in front of her.

"And if you believe her," Libby chimed in. "I've got a piece of the Mackinac Bridge I can sell you."

"Libby, you're not making this any easier, you know."

She grinned. "I know. But I wasn't aware I was supposed to." She blew an air kiss to Alyssa. "Love ya, Lys."

"Well, that's debatable," Alyssa muttered.

"Oh, come now, Alyssa dear. Libby is obviously just excited about whatever happened last night."

"Right," Libby replied. "And I know your grandmother will be, too. So will you tell her already? Before I do."

Alyssa swallowed once and wet her lips. "Scott kissed me last night."

Grandma raised one eyebrow. "Did he now?"

"Yes." Even talking about it brought back the tingle to her lips. Alyssa reached up and touched her mouth. It didn't take much to bring the vision of Scott's face to mind either.

"How nice, dear."

"Oh, it was more than nice," Libby exclaimed. "It had our dear Lys completely addlepated for the rest of the evening." She giggled. "She almost bumped into a wall on the way back to our room, too."

Alyssa looked across to the sofa opposite her and caught her friend's attention. "You seem to know what happened so well, why don't you tell the story."

"Really, Lys? Can I?"

Alyssa waved her hand at Libby in a dismissing fashion. "Be my guest."

"Oh, Mrs. Denham, it was great." Libby laid down her quilt pieces and bounced in her seat. "I was standing with Lys when Scott arrived, and then I left them alone and took a seat in one of the rocking chairs on the porch."

"So, this kiss took place on the porch at the hotel?" Grandma didn't even look up.

"Yes," Libby replied. "Near the west end."

"Hmm, it's the same place where Alyssa's parents kissed for the first time, too."

Alyssa snapped her head up. "My parents?"

"It is?" Libby added.

Grandma nodded. "Yes. Now, it happened over thirty years ago, but I believe it's where your father said it was." She pressed her lips into a thin line and furrowed her brows. "Yes, it was. The west end of the porch. I'm certain of it."

"Why have I never heard this story before?" She'd begged Dad to tell her everything about his meeting Mom and their dating relationship, and he had. All of it, leading up to when he'd proposed by the lighthouse on the island. She'd heard the story so many times, it played in her mind like a movie. But he'd never said anything about their first kiss being at the hotel.

"I don't know, dear. Your father never talked much about such things." She smiled. "It was your grandfather who managed to pry the information out of him one night. And even then, it wasn't much. Just a bit about his nervousness, how things hadn't gone according to plan, and how he was glad he could put it behind him."

"Dad had a plan for kissing Mom for the first time?" Alyssa tilted her head. "It sounds a little like Scott last night."

"I'm finished with these two pieces," Libby said, holding up her handiwork. She must have gone back to stitching when the telling of the story shifted.

Grandma glanced over at her. "And you've remembered to press the seam open and flat? Excellent." She reached down beside her and produced another piece of fabric. "Here is another one you can add to what you have." Grandma turned back to Alyssa. "Now, dear, what's this about Scott's plan?"

"Oh, I don't know if he actually had one," Alyssa replied. "But it sure seems like he did the more I think about it. I mean, he did invite me after church yesterday morning to join him on the porch in the evening. So, it certainly wasn't random." And the way he'd guided the conversation from one topic to the next. It couldn't have been without any forethought at all.

"Well, he certainly intended to speak with you last night, dear," Grandma said. "But no one can perfectly plan anything when another person is involved. We all have a way of doing our own thing, and it almost always ends up being at odds with whatever plans the other person might have." She pulled her needle up through the fabric until the thread was taut and sent it diving back through the material again. "It's why we have to leave some things up to God and not attempt to control everything. His plans are always the best, no matter what we might think."

Control. Alyssa had been doing it for years. Controlling her environment, her relationships, her career path. Everything. And where had it gotten her? Alone and lacking any real fun in her life. Just like what Libby had accused her of months ago.

"Well, I knew this entire trip was a God-thing from the start. I just never expected anything like what's happened." She expelled a full breath. "Especially not with Scott."

Grandma fought hard to keep the smile from spreading across her face. "Upset your ordered little world, did he, dear?"

"You can say that again," Libby answered with a grin. "Lys couldn't walk straight, much less talk last night." Mischief lit up her face. "I think it's a good thing Scott called me over to take his place, or Lys might've fallen right then and there from going weak at the knees."

"It was not so bad, Lib." Alyssa shook her head. "You're exaggerating again."

"Am not!" She gave Alyssa a pointed look. "You should've seen yourself as Scott walked away. You were definitely gone."

Alyssa couldn't deny she'd struggled to breathe, let alone stand. So, she couldn't lie about it. "Well, what do you expect?" She returned Libby's knowing stare. "Wouldn't you have done the same thing if you'd been kissed like that?"

"Oh, I would've fallen right there on the porch if I'd been in your shoes." She laughed. "And I probably would have done it before he'd even left." Libby turned to Grandma. "Mrs. Denham, you should've been there. It was the most romantic thing I'd ever seen. Definitely movie-worthy material."

Grandma's eyebrows rose. "It certainly sounds like it." She looked at Alyssa. "Dear, it appears you and your mother have even more in common than you might've thought." She smiled. "You might want to give her a call when you get home. Sit down with her and compare notes. Perhaps it will help you with whatever your dear Scott has planned."

Your dear Scott. My dear Scott. Either one had a nice ring to it. As for plans, did he have any beyond last night's kiss? Alyssa had no idea. Only five days remained of their vacation, and then she'd go back to her world, and he'd remain here in his. What kind of plans could happen with an entire state in between them?

A knock sounded at the door.

Grandma looked up. "Here's your ride for your next visit."

Alyssa's heart skipped a beat. Scott! She fussed with the creases in her capris, tugged on the bottom of her sleeveless button-down top, and fluffed her hair.

"You look beautiful, dear," Grandma said with a soft smile. She pointed to each of the pieces they already had and moved her mouth as she silently counted out the blocks. "Two of the ladies no longer live here on the island, so they had theirs sent over, and Margaret Doud mailed hers. She's the mayor of the island, so I'm not surprised. The packages were all waiting for me on Saturday. So, it leaves us with just one more after today."

Only one more. Alyssa sighed. So much had happened in such a short time. And now it was all coming to a close.

Libby danced across the floor toward to the window and peered through the sheer curtain then continued her sashay to the front door. "Ah, if it isn't our island knight in shining armor come to whisk away our fair damsel on another quilt block adventure."

Alyssa's heart pounded now. Should she stand up and greet him or wait for him to come in? Should she rush and beat Libby to the door? No. It would make her look too eager. Let Libby do the honors. Alyssa dried her hands on her pants and took several deep breaths.

"Just be yourself, Alyssa dear," Grandma advised. "Remember. Scott likes you for who you are. So, relax and have a good time. And as difficult as I know this will be for you, try to go with the flow."

Hearing such a phrase come from her grandmother sounded so odd. Maybe she'd been taking lessons from Libby. Alyssa smiled. "Thank you."

"Scott!" Libby's voice carried across the room. "Nice to see you this morning. Did you sleep good last night?"

Oh no! Alyssa winced. Why did Libby have to meddle so much?

"As a matter of fact, I did," Scott replied. "You?"

"Yes. So, I guess only one of us had trouble."

Scott's footsteps thudded on the hardwood floor, and a moment later, he stood behind the sofa opposite Grandma. "Miss Edith, good morning. Sorry I'm late, but I had a little issue with the harness and the horse."

"You're here now, though," Grandma replied. "And it's all that matters."

"Hello, Alyssa."

His voice had changed just slightly, and the gentle inflection wafted over Alyssa. She wet her lips and took another breath before raising her gaze to meet his. Oh, if only her heart would stop beating so fast, she might be able to find her voice to answer him. She opened her mouth, but no words came out. His mouth slid into a soft smile.

"Are you ready to go?"

"Yes," she managed to whisper. She placed her hands on the sofa cushion where she sat and prayed her feet would support her. As soon as she stood, Scott was right there with his hand outstretched.

"Allow me," he said and held onto her fingers, helping her to her feet. Scott led her around the sofa and toward the front door where Libby waited. He glanced back over his shoulder. "Have a nice morning, Miss Edith." He tucked Alyssa's hand into the crook of his elbow. "I promise to take good care of these ladies."

"Oh, I have no doubt, Scott." Grandma's voice held a hint of amusement. "Enjoy your visit with Mrs. Musser."

Scott drove the carriage up Grand Avenue and stopped under the portico in front of the Grand Hotel.

Alyssa glanced at the red-carpeted stairs and the two footmen who stepped up to assist her and Libby from the carriage. "Why have we stopped here?"

"You said Mrs. Musser, right?" Scott hopped down and joined them. "Mrs. Amelia Musser?"

"Yes."

He gestured toward the hotel. "She spends most of her time here." Scott placed his hands at the backs of both Alyssa and Libby, and they walked with him up the stairs. "Her husband passed away just last year, and her son is the current owner of the hotel. She's often said the hotel is like her home, and those who stay here are her personal guests. Makes her feel responsible for them in some way, so she does everything she can to help them feel comfortable."

They reached the top, and Alyssa stopped. "Wait a minute. Musser? As in Dan Musser?" She tapped her forehead. "Now I remember. My father and grandmother used to tell me stories about the Musser family and how they were pretty much a permanent fixture here. I think I've even met Mrs. Musser before."

"Well, I guess you're about to find out," Scott replied. "We'll likely find her in the Parlor if she's not out walking Sadie, their little Scottish terrier."

"You know," Libby spoke up. "Why don't you two go ahead and meet with Mrs. Musser? I think I'm going to go see if I can find Ben and stir up a little trouble."

"Are you sure?" Alyssa asked. History wasn't exactly Libby's thing, but skipping out on talking with a woman who probably had dozens of fascinating stories to share didn't seem like her at all.

"Positive." She shooed them away. "Go on. Have fun. You can fill me in on all the details later. I've got a certain events coordinator to track down." She walked off with a wave of her hand over her head. "Toodles!"

"Guess it's just us," Scott said, looking down at her with a smile.

"Guess so." Alyssa shrugged. "Let's go find Mrs. Musser."

They headed inside and straight to the front desk. Scott exchanged a few words with the clerk, who pointed, and he nodded.

"All right," Scott said, joining Alyssa again. "Amelia is in the Parlor, as I suspected. It's this way."

The elegant room looked just the same as it did the last time Alyssa had been there. Longer than it was wide, with white square pillars lining both sides of the main walkway. Red velvet wingback chairs sat in front of each of the pillars on one side of the room, and large ferns helped afford a sense of privacy. They walked across a plush, navy blue carpet with red geranium bouquets and small green lilac bushes in a squared pattern. Several golden chandeliers hung from the ceiling, and the far wall featured a mural of a Mackinac Island scene.

"There she is," Scott said suddenly.

Alyssa followed his gaze to a glass table in the corner adorned with a substantial flower bouquet in a crystal vase at its center. She walked next to Scott as they approached the table, and the woman seated there looked up. The Scottish terrier in her lap also popped up her head and regarded them with curious eyes.

"Alyssa Denham," the woman said with a smile, her voice smooth and cultured, as she held out her hand. Her silver hair fell from a center part straight to her shoulders, and a pair of black glasses framed her face. "It's so nice to see you again, dear. Been a long time."

"Mrs. Musser," Alyssa replied, accepting her handshake.

"Please, call me Amelia." She grinned up at Scott and stroked the ears of her dog. "All the employees and guests do." Amelia nodded. "How are you, Scott?" She nodded at Alyssa. "Have you added personal escort to your long list of job responsibilities, or is this someone special?"

He actually blushed under Amelia's amused stare. Then, his arm slipped around Alyssa's waist, and he pulled her close. "Definitely someone special," he replied. "Although it didn't start out that way. Miss Edith hired me to escort her granddaughter around the island on a personal quest, and well . . ." He glanced down at Alyssa. "I guess it turned into more."

"Please sit," Amelia invited. "I'd like to hear all about this quest from Edith. She phoned not too long ago to say you were coming for a visit, and she'd be sure to send you here to speak with me."

Scott slid the vase toward one end of the table and held out a chair for Alyssa. "I told Alyssa about Dan's passing last year," he said as soon as he was seated.

"Yes," Alyssa added. "I'm so sorry for your loss."

Amelia's eyes glistened, and she sniffed. "Not just my loss, dear, but a loss to this hotel, the island, and a greater part of the tourism industry in this state." Pride gleamed from her face. "Dan had worked at this hotel from the ground up for nearly sixty years. He loved it here, as a kid when he visited and as an employee when his Uncle Stewart hired him. His passion directly affected how he ran this hotel as both a president and then owner."

"I remember the stories my grandmother told me about running up and down the porch with your husband when they were kids. And my father mentioned Mr. Musser more than once when he talked about bringing clients here for business lunches."

Amelia stroked Sadie's ears again, and the dog snuggled into Amelia's lap. "Dan was always involved with all the guests. When we redesigned the hotel's interior during America's bicentennial, Dan insisted on being hands-on with just about everything." She chuckled. "Of course, the architect and decorator we hired didn't always agree with his suggestions, but they did an amazing job just the same." She made a sweeping gesture with one hand around the room. "It's thanks to Mr. Bos and Mr. Varney no two rooms in this hotel are alike, and the concept was my husband's suggestion."

"He's left quite a legacy, for sure." Alyssa shook her head. "And with your son as the president now, it looks as if the legacy is continuing." Grandma knew some influential people on this island.

But after living here all her life, she would. To think, the hotel owner's wife was a part of a quilting group.

"Yes. Just last year we marked eighty years of our family ownership of the Grand. It started with Dan's uncle, then shifted to our family when Dan and I purchased the hotel the same year they filmed *Somewhere in Time* here." She looked at both Alyssa and Scott. "Are either of you familiar with the film?"

Scott laughed. "Oh, yes. Alyssa knows it well."

Amelia raised her eyebrows. "Wait a moment. Don't tell me you're one of the hundreds of fans who come here every October for the convention, are you?"

"No," Alyssa replied. "Though I've wanted for a while to be here then." She shrugged. "My parents are named Richard and Elise, but not after the film," she added.

"And it gets better," Scott stated. "Her middle name is McKenna."

Amelia smiled. "Well, you *do* know the film, dear. Seems like your family is as tied to it as mine is to this hotel. Speaking of which," she began as she reached into a tote next to her. "I believe you have come to collect these?" she said, passing two completed blocks across the table to Alyssa.

"Yes. We were just assembling the quilt earlier this morning at my grandmother's cottage."

"I must admit, when Edith phoned with the details of this project, I had my doubts it would ever come to fruition. The original ladies are so spread out it seems, and some of us haven't spoken to each other in years." Amelia laid her hand flat on the table, her fingers pointing toward the pieces Alyssa now held. "But it sounds as if it's coming together nicely. Tell me, how far along are you?"

"Well, Grandma said this morning we had only one more block to collect, and then we could piece it all together and get the backing on." She grinned. "I'm not much of a quilter, or a sewer of any kind, so I'm not sure I even have all the terminology right."

Amelia smiled. "Oh, you do, dear. Edith obviously has been teaching you while you're visiting. I am impressed."

"I'll tell Grandma when we get back to the cottage."

"And tell her I'd love for her to come visit. We can catch up on old times." A distant look entered her eyes. "It's been far too long."

Alyssa nodded. "I will."

A tiny whine came from Sadie, and Amelia glanced down at her dog. "It appears my little trophy gal needs to go for a walk." She gently set the dog on the floor and started to rise, but Scott jumped to help her. "Thank you," she said, accepting his assistance and nodding toward the tote. "Alyssa, would you be a dear and grab my bag for me? We can go together to the front desk where you can leave it until I return from the walk."

"Sure," Alyssa said and stepped around the other side of the table to grab the tote.

"Shall we?" Scott extended his elbow to Amelia and silently gestured to Alyssa to join him on his other side.

The three of them—no, make it four with Sadie—walked through the Parlor toward the main entrance. Amelia paused to ask the clerk to take her tote then turned toward Alyssa and Scott.

"You take good care of her, now, Scott," she admonished with a wink. "Or I might have to report you to my son."

Scott grinned. "Yes, ma'am."

Amelia looked at Alyssa. "And again, dear, give my regards to your grandmother."

Such grace and charm and a genuine concern for others. No wonder she'd managed to hang onto the hotel for so long. Alyssa could learn a lot from a woman like Amelia.

"Come on," Scott said, placing his hand about her waist and guiding her toward the elevator. "I have about an hour before I have to start my shift here. Let's get something to eat."

14

I can't believe Libby and I are leaving tomorrow," Alyssa said with a cute little pout on her lips. She pushed her spoon around one end of the dog-bone-shaped bowl of the Grand Sundae Scott had ordered for them to share. "The time has gone so fast. It's going to be so hard to leave this place."

Yes, hard for him, too. But he had to be strong for them both. "At least we can enjoy a few special things before then." Scott glanced around Sadie's Ice Cream Parlor and smiled. "I've wanted to check out this place since it opened last year but never had the chance." He tipped his chin a little. "Or the right company."

Alyssa looked around the room at the décor. "This is a stunning layout. Carleton Varney has outdone himself again. The round white marble tables, the twisted iron chairs, the red-and-white-striped window valances, the lanterns on the pillars. Even the semicircle construction blends perfectly with the rest of the hotel." She took a bite of ice cream. "And this blueberry cobbler flavor is delicious!" Alyssa slid the spoon from her mouth and went back to lick the leftovers. "I admit, I've been weak and gone with the store-bought ice cream back home. Hudsonville's is probably all over Grand Rapids." She gave him a sheepish grin. "But I've been lazy about picking it up."

Scott reached across their little round table and placed his hand on her wrist. "Then, I'm doubly glad I get to share this experience with you."

"After meeting Sadie on Monday, it's fun to see her get her own ice cream parlor named after her." She giggled. "My most favorite part, though, is the framed cartoon wall hangings, especially the one of little Sadie licking her own cone."

He raised his eyebrows. "It's your *favorite* part of this afternoon?"

"Of course," she replied with a straight face. "What else could it be?"

Scott narrowed his eyes. Was she teasing him, or did he just need to work on impressing her better? He didn't get a chance to ask, though. Two security guards approached their little table.

"Alyssa Denham?" the one on the left asked. Scott didn't know him.

"Yes?" Alyssa replied.

"I'm going to have to ask you to come with us." He glanced at Scott. "And you, too, Mr. Whitman."

Scott glanced at the other guard, who stood with an expression of regret on his face. "What's this all about, Ted?"

"I'm sorry, Scott, but I can't say anything right now. Just come with us."

Alyssa slid off the vinyl bench seat and stepped around the table. Scott stood and immediately reached for her hand, giving it a squeeze. She looked at him, and he shrugged. "Guess our ice cream will have to wait."

In silence, the four of them walked through the parlor and into the hall outside the rest of the shops on the ground floor. They took the rear stairs to the main floor and entered the hallway across from the security director's office. Jason met them at the door.

"Scott." He nodded. "I wish this meeting was under better circumstances." Jason stepped aside and beckoned everyone to enter. He waved away the two guards.

Ted gave Scott a firm handshake before he left with the other guard. "I know you didn't do anything. I'm pulling for ya."

"Thank you," Scott replied.

"Oh, Alyssa dear!" Amelia stood as soon as they entered, holding tight to Sadie. "I'm so sorry you've been dragged into all of this. I've told Jason here there must be some mistake. You two couldn't possibly be involved." She reached for Alyssa's hand. "But he says they have an eyewitness who can prove it. And he's the grandson of a rather wealthy investor in the hotel. So, of course, they had to call you both in."

"Call us in about what?" Alyssa asked.

Scott wanted to know the same thing. Eyewitness? Wealthy investor? Involved in something? None of this made sense. What in the world was going on?

"Mrs. Musser," Jason spoke in a calm voice, staying her long-winded protest with his hand. "If you'd let me explain, I'm sure we can get all of this cleared up." He moved behind his desk and picked up some papers, then flipped through them, giving each one a quick perusal. Glancing up, he nodded toward the two chairs opposite. "Please be seated."

Amelia resumed her seat, cradling Sadie in her lap. Scott gestured toward the other chair and allowed Alyssa to sit. He stood behind her and placed his hands on her shoulders, giving them a little massage.

"Now," Jason began, running his fingers from the sides of his mouth to his chin. "It says here, Scott, you and Alyssa were with Mrs. Musser on Monday." He looked at them both. "True?"

"Yes," Scott replied. "We met her in the Parlor for about thirty minutes not long before lunch, then walked with her into the lobby when she had to take Sadie for a walk."

"Good. Exactly what Mrs. Musser said." Jason laid one sheet of paper down and made some notations on it. "Now, Miss Denham." The director turned his attention to Alyssa. "Did you also come into contact with a certain floral tote during your visit with Mrs. Musser?"

Alyssa tilted her head. "Yes. It was sitting on the floor next to her chair in the Parlor, and she asked me to help her take it to the registration counter. She said they would keep it there for her until she returned from her walk."

"Hmm." Jason pressed his lips firm then sighed. "Your statements match up exactly with what Mrs. Musser reported. It seems Mrs. Musser has misplaced a jewelry case with an anniversary brooch pinned inside, and you two were the last ones to have been in contact with the tote just before she noticed it missing."

"But Jason," Scott began. "How could we have known the brooch was even in the tote when we were only with Amelia for less than thirty minutes? And we literally walked from the Parlor to the front room. That's it. When would there have been time to lift a case we didn't know was there, from a tote we'd only held for a couple of minutes, before giving it to the clerk on duty?"

Jason laid the papers on his desk, then he scrubbed at his eyes and ran his hands through his hair. "I don't know," he groaned. "I'm just trying to figure out this mess and get to the bottom of things."

"Do you see, Jason?" Mrs. Musser spoke again. "I told you these two couldn't possibly have done what this witness claims."

The witness again. And Jason had yet to even give them a name. He'd only mentioned some wealthy investor's grandson. Scott knew most of the families who had a vested interest in the hotel, and not a single one of them had any reason to stir up trouble like this. He looked down at Alyssa, who fidgeted with her fingers, twisting them. She was nervous. And he was, too. But he couldn't let her see it. Not exactly how he'd thought he'd be spending his last day with her.

Scott got Jason's attention again. "If we weren't with Amelia more than thirty minutes, and no one else was around us, how could this witness have seen what he says he saw?"

Jason looked again at Amelia. "Mrs. Musser, are you certain you had the brooch in the tote just before you visited with Scott and Miss Denham?"

"Yes." Amelia gave one succinct nod. "I had a meeting just after lunch with a reporter from the *Chicago Sun-Times*, and she'd requested a picture of it for the article. So, I had it brought out from the hotel safe and placed it in my tote before going to the Parlor."

"And no one else besides Ted saw you with the case or knew it was in your tote?"

Amelia tapped her lips with her index finger. "Well, there was this young man I bumped into as I turned from the front desk. He was so polite." She stroked Sadie's head. "Even petted Sadie here and wished me a nice day."

Ah, now they were getting somewhere. Scott opened his mouth, but Jason beat him to it.

"Did you happen to recognize him? Get a name, a description, or anything?"

"Oh, I don't need a description. He's Maureen Corbitt's grandson. A sweet young man."

"I'm sorry," Alyssa spoke up, her voice strained. "Did you say Maureen Corbitt?"

Scott tensed his grip on Alyssa's shoulders. The woman Miss Dottie had mentioned last week. The one who took over for Miss Edith without being asked to do so.

Amelia turned toward Alyssa. "Yes, dear. An old and beloved friend." She snapped her fingers. "And a member of our quilting circle, too. Has she given you *her* contribution to the quilt you're making?"

"We met with her on Tuesday," Alyssa replied. "She was waiting on her front porch, and we didn't stay long."

The whole meeting had been cold and awkward. If anyone had a beef with Alyssa or her family, it'd be her. But it still didn't explain her grandson. She wouldn't put her own family in the middle of this petty feud, would she?

Jason consulted the papers in the report again. "This young man's name wouldn't happen to be Charlie, would it?"

Amelia smiled at him. "Why yes! Yes, it was."

Alyssa shuddered, and Scott squeezed her shoulders a little too hard. She winced, and he relaxed his grip. Charlie Jarman. Scott hadn't seen him anywhere around the hotel since the fight. And now he knew why. The lowlife had been skulking around looking for a way to nab them.

The director sighed. "And there we have it. The man is Charlie Jarman." Jason looked at Alyssa and Scott. "Do either of you know him?"

"Yes," Alyssa said, her voice meek and soft. She reached up and touched Scott's hand on her shoulder, and he threaded his fingers through hers.

And you'll pay for this. Charlie's parting words to Scott after their fight came back to him. Looks like he'd found a way to seek revenge.

"We, uh, ran into him a few days ago," Scott replied. "And I'm afraid things didn't go so well." He put it mildly. But Scott didn't want to give out the details if he didn't have to. Alyssa had been through enough with the slimy scumbag.

"So you're saying I should investigate him a little more and see if he might be the man we're looking for?"

Scott grimaced. "I hate to say it, but yeah."

"Okay." Jason tapped the papers into a neat stack, set them down, then closed the folder. "Looks like we won't be needing the three of you anymore." He moved from behind his desk and opened his office door. "You're free to go."

Alyssa released a long breath, and her shoulders slumped. Thank God for small miracles. Scott gave her hand a squeeze as Amelia stood and situated Sadie in her arms. The smile she gave the two of them showed her remorse.

"Please accept my apology. Both of you." Amelia reached for Alyssa's free hand. "And please come back and visit anytime. I'll make certain you have one of our best suites."

"Thank you." Alyssa withdrew her hand from Scott's and embraced the proprietress of the hotel.

Amelia left the director's office ahead of them, and Scott nodded at Jason as they passed. He paused with Alyssa in the hallway and turned to face her.

"Well, this was a little extra excitement for our day," he said, forcing brightness into his voice.

She closed her eyes and pressed her fingers to her temples. "One I hope we don't have to repeat."

Scott cradled her face in his hands, and she lowered hers to her sides, staring up at him with unshed tears. "I'll make sure of it." He leaned down and placed a quick kiss on her lips. "Now, how about we go meet your grandmother? We'll only be a little late, if we hurry."

<hr />

"I can't believe Charlie would hide behind his grandmother's skirt and accuse the two of you of something like this." Grandma paced back and forth across her living room. "It makes me so mad." She threw her hands in the air and expelled her breath. "And on your last day here, too. I had hoped this time would be much more special, not marred by false accusations and meetings with hotel security."

"How did you figure it out?" Libby asked from her seat on the sofa across from them.

"It took a bit of doing," Scott replied. "But the security director asked enough questions for almost all the pieces to come together. And when they did, we supplied the final piece."

"I'm sure Maureen didn't know a thing about this," Grandma said. "Charlie just used his relation to her to get what he wanted. The little wretch. I'm sorry I ever gave him cookies and milk on my front porch all those years ago."

"Grandma," Alyssa said softly. "It's all right. And you know you're not sorry about being nice to him. No one could've known things would turn out like this." She smiled at Scott, seated next to her on the sofa, before turning her attention back to her grandmother. "Scott and I had a little chat on the way over here. It wasn't exactly the way we thought it would happen, but at least we're able to have closure with this whole Charlie mess."

"And we can all move past it to much better things," Scott added. "Life's a grand adventure, and we're all just along for the ride."

"And speaking of better things . . ." Grandma walked to the corner of the room and lifted a square package into her arms. "I called all three of you here this afternoon for a special presentation." She stepped around the coffee table and handed the package to Alyssa. "This is for you, my dear."

Alyssa looked down at the package wrapped with a satin ribbon and a bow tied on top. Archival paper! The same thing they'd wrapped around the Friendship Quilt they'd finished yesterday. She smoothed her fingers over the satin and looked up at her grandmother. "Grandma, what have you done?"

"Open it and find out."

Libby scooted to the edge of the sofa, and Scott shifted in his seat to angle toward Alyssa. Grandma perched on the edge of the coffee table and folded her hands in her lap. Everyone waited for her to reveal what was inside.

With painstaking slowness, Alyssa untied the ribbon and unwound it from the package. Then, she pulled away each corner of the first layer of paper before removing it and starting on the second layer. One more layer greeted her under it, and Alyssa gave her grandmother a questioning glance.

"You wanted to make the package secure, didn't you, Mrs. Denham?" Libby asked.

Grandma smiled. "I didn't want anything to happen to it. No stains, no threads unraveling, nothing." She gestured toward the package. "It's the last layer, I promise."

Alyssa folded back the paper to reveal the quilt she, Libby, and Grandma had worked so hard and fast to complete just last night. They'd assembled, basted, stitched, and stretched until the quilt took on its final shape. And now it sat in Alyssa's lap, a priceless gift from a beloved person. Tears welled up in Alyssa's eyes as she ran her hands across the section she could see.

"Oh, Grandma," she said, raising her eyes to meet her grandmother's. "You shouldn't have done this."

"This whole project was meant just for you, Alyssa dear." Grandma reached across and covered Alyssa's hand with hers. "Sure, it started out as a dream of mine, but once you arrived and started helping me, I knew who needed the quilt."

"Oh, Lys!" Libby exclaimed. "It's going to look fantastic on the wall in your living room. The colors match perfectly!"

"Grandma, are you sure about this?" Alyssa loved the quilt, but she didn't want to take away her grandmother's dream. "These blocks and squares represent all those years you spent with the ladies in your circle and all those memories you made along the way."

"Exactly right, dear. And all those memories were made because our little circle made a promise to stick together, no matter what." She leaned back and placed her hands on the table. "We celebrated birthdays, anniversaries, weddings, friends moving away, friends passing away, and a lot of little things, too. But through it all, together, we made those memories last." Grandma nodded at the quilt. "And now, you can take those memories with you to remind you of the special times you can celebrate in your own life." She dipped her chin and gave Alyssa a knowing look. "If you're willing to trust God and open up your heart to let others in."

Trust. Yes, she hadn't done a good job of it in a long while. But if she learned anything on this little vacation, it was opening up her heart and letting others in made all the difference in the world.

"I will." Alyssa nodded. "But only if you promise me one thing."

"What is it, dear?"

"You will stop avoiding those people in your life who mean a lot to you, and accept their invitations to tea, to visit, whatever?" Alyssa held her grandmother's hands in hers. "I found my healing here these past two weeks, and you need to do the same." She touched her forehead to Grandma's. "Sixteen years is a long time to let fear and hurt dictate your life." She smiled. "I should know."

Tears pooled in her grandmother's eyes, and answering ones gathered in Alyssa's as well. Scott grabbed the quilt and slid it onto his lap, and Alyssa leaned forward to embrace Grandma. They held tight for several moments before her grandmother pulled back and smiled.

"I promise, dear." She sniffed and straightened, then stood. "All right. Enough of this melancholy atmosphere," Grandma stated. "I've got a roast in the oven, some fresh-baked bread, and a scrumptious apple-pear strudel with caramel sabayon, courtesy of our fine chefs at the Grand Hotel." She clapped her hands and headed for the kitchen. "Let's make the most of this last night together, shall we?"

Alyssa pressed her lips closed and breathed through her nose. She wouldn't cry. She couldn't. Scott wouldn't want their last moments together to be sad. And she didn't want to leave him with the memory of her tear-streaked face. She straightened and inhaled a cleansing breath as Scott loaded her luggage into the boat. Ben had already hopped in with Libby, leaving the two of them standing on the dock. They'd agreed he wouldn't go across the lake with them, as it was hard enough already.

With the last bag stowed, Scott dusted off his hands and turned to face her. He swallowed once, and his Adam's apple bounced. Alyssa refused to be the one to make this farewell any more difficult. Scott licked his lips and closed the distance between them, immediately reaching for her hands, which he raised and held close to his chest.

"I know we said our good-byes last night, and we agreed we wouldn't drag this out today." Scott closed his eyes and placed a kiss on her thumbs. When he opened his eyes, the sheen of tears glistened in the sunlight. "But I also can't send you off without saying how much I'm going to miss you."

"And I you," Alyssa whispered.

"Neither one of us knows what's going to happen tomorrow." He removed one of his hands and reached into his pocket, bringing out a small envelope with her name written on it. "And until then, I wanted to give you this to remember me by."

Alyssa took the envelope and started to open it. But Scott stopped her.

"No," he said softly. "Wait until you get home." He grinned and swallowed again. "It won't have the same effect unless you do."

"Okay." She took the card and slipped it into her purse.

"Now, come here," he said, pulling her to him. "I have one more thing I'd like to give you."

———— ⌘ ————

"You watch her from a distance long enough, and you might end up watching her head right out of your life."

Scott turned at Miss Edith's words. When had she gotten herself down from the carriage and come down to the docks?

She elbowed him. "What are you waiting for? If you love her, tell her."

Scott stared out across the lake at the vanishing speedboat. "It's too late."

"It's never too late."

But could Alyssa be happy with him? With life on this island? She'd been in the big city for most of her life, and though she'd spent many summers on the island, her life was there in Grand Rapids. Sure, he already felt her absence. But it wasn't all about him. He wanted Alyssa to be happy, in the choices she made for her life. And as difficult as it was to admit it . . . even if her life was without him.

"Well, I left her with a note and my sincerest wish tucked inside." He sighed. "It's up to her now."

Alyssa stared out the window of the train as it sped away from Mackinaw City and headed for Grand Rapids. Libby patted her hand and gave her a sympathetic smile, then turned her attention back to her fashion magazine. Alyssa held out the bag of fudge to her friend. Libby smiled and took a handful of pieces, immediately taking a bite. She'd had to say good-bye, too, and though she put up a brave front, walking away from Ben hadn't been easy either.

But life continued, whether they liked it or not. Alyssa bit into her own piece of fudge. And they both had their lives back home. Even as thoughts plagued her mind of the piles of work she was sure awaited her, Alyssa couldn't get Scott out of her head. He'd pushed through her self-erected walls and broken into her inner sanctum, a place where she'd only allowed her family and Libby to be. And he'd patiently held her hand as she'd stepped into uncharted territory. No one else had ever been willing to do it. At least, no one else she'd ever been willing to *let* do it. Now, Scott was gone, and she was alone again.

Alyssa retrieved the envelope from her purse and opened it, and then she slid out the folded note. Scott told her not to read it until she got home, but she couldn't resist. She already missed him, and though they promised to write and call, she'd left a piece of her heart with him back on the island. If she couldn't have him right now, at least she could have his words to comfort her. She unfolded the note and read.

The card had only one line written inside it. "Come back to me."

15

Scott roamed the hotel, floor by floor. Then, he paced the entire length of the front porch . . . twice. This place wasn't the same without Alyssa. His work continued, and he spent each day escorting hotel visitors from the dock to the hotel and all around the island. But his rehearsed speeches lacked the passion they once had. Or maybe he'd just found something better, and this paled now in comparison.

Is this what his life had been like before Alyssa arrived?

He missed the lilt of her voice, her soft smile, her skittish hesitancy, and the effortless way her cinnamon hair settled about her shoulders. It was hard to believe he'd only known her for two weeks. In the short time, he'd learned more about Alyssa than all of the people who'd worked around him for years. Even more than he knew about Ben, and they'd been friends since they were teens. He'd also told Alyssa more about himself than he'd told anyone else.

How could someone come and upset everything so thoroughly in just fourteen days?

Scott pressed the button on the espresso machine and waited for his cup to fill. This lack of sleep was getting to him. He should have told Alyssa how he felt about her. Should have told her he loved her.

Instead of leaving just one line in the card. What if she didn't come back? She had let fourteen years pass from her last visit. Would she do it again?

"I hope she gets back soon." Ben poked his head into the employee break room. "I don't know how much more of your moping I can take."

Scott looked over at his friend. "I'm not moping."

"You are, too. You're like a little lost puppy dog. If you don't tell her how you feel when she gets back, I will." Ben slapped the door frame with his palm and left.

If she comes back.

Every day they chatted online or exchanged emails was one more day closer to when Scott was going to pack his bags and head to Grand Rapids to see her. They hadn't spoken on the phone, and it was his doing. He didn't trust himself not to bring up the note and if she'd read it yet or if she'd decided what to do. It had to be her choice, and he didn't want to influence her in any way.

Scott took a swig of his espresso, the hot liquid searing down his throat. He set the cup in the sink and ran water in it. There. Now he could get back to work. Maybe one of these times, he'd get so busy, he wouldn't have time to think about Alyssa.

"The Grand Hotel, please," Alyssa told the driver as soon as one of the ferry attendants had loaded her one bag.

Quite a difference from her last arrival to this island a little over a month ago. Today, the cooler September temperatures brought a brisk breeze blowing off the lake. Alyssa pulled the sweater of her dress tighter around her to ward off the chill. She leaned against the seat back and relaxed to the familiar clip-clop of the horses' hooves. The lapping of the lake water against the island's shore faded in the distance as the carriage made its way down Market Street and turned north on Cadotte as it climbed to Bluff Road.

In typical fashion, the carriage slowed to a stop under the porch overhang, and a waiting attendant set the stepping block down for her. Alyssa scooted forward and placed her hands on either side of the opening.

"I'll take over from here, George," a familiar voice said.

"Ben?" If he was here to greet her, it meant . . . "Where's Scott?" she asked.

Without answering, Ben held out his hand and helped her down from the carriage. He signaled to the driver to be on his way. When she thought he'd lead her toward the red carpet, Ben turned her around instead.

At the sight of the second carriage, Alyssa stopped short and gave a heavy sigh. "I'm not going." She covered a yawn and shook her head. "No."

Ben looked at her and back at the carriage. "You have to."

"No, I don't." She turned back toward the stairs and the waiting attendant who stood with her bag. That path looked far more inviting than yet another ride somewhere. After a taxi, a train, another taxi, a ferry, and a carriage, she was done. And in spite of all of it, Scott wasn't even here to greet her.

Ben stepped in front of her. "Please. If you don't, I—I—"

"You'll what?"

"I'll lose my job."

She rolled her eyes. "There's no way you could lose your job because I won't take a carriage ride to who knows where."

Ben knelt down and pressed his hands together, giving her a pleading look and looking quite pathetic. "Please. Do me this one favor."

"But I'm exhausted, Ben. I've been traveling all day." She nodded toward the hotel. "And I know there's a soft bed up there calling my name." She didn't want to share her disappointment at not seeing the one person she'd traveled all day to see. He hadn't bothered to greet her here, let alone down at the dock. "I don't want to go."

"You don't know what a bad position I'm in. If you don't go, I'll pick you up and carry you to the carriage. It'll solve your exhaustion. All you have to do is sit." He took her hand and pulled her to the waiting carriage. "Come on, you can do it. One foot in front of the other."

"You know, you're annoying."

Ben gave her a fake smile. "And proud of it. And I'll continue to be annoying until you get into the carriage."

What was the use? She heaved a big sigh. She took Ben's hand to steady herself and stepped aboard. "I want my hat, please."

"I'll be right back." Ben returned quickly and handed her hat to her with a bow and a circular wave of his hand. "Driver, you may go now."

Alyssa set her floppy hat on her head and leaned back against the plush seat. The carriage lurched forward and made a wide turn just past the hotel. It headed back in the direction from which it came and wound its way down Cadotte Avenue toward the water. She gazed up at the blue sky and all the white, puffy clouds reminded her of how good it would feel to sink into the billowy softness of a custom mattress.

"Driver, stop."

He pulled on the reins, and the horses eased the carriage to a halt.

She sighed. "Please, take me back to the hotel."

The driver turned in his seat and took off his top hat. "But we're almost there," he said with a big grin.

"Scott!" She hadn't expected this. So he *had* been there all along. "This was all your idea?"

"Who else's would it be?"

She shrugged.

"So you're not disappointed?"

Her mouth pulled into a smile. "Not at all. Tired. But not disappointed. Not now, anyway."

"Can I continue our little drive then?"

"Of course."

He snapped the reins and drove farther down Cadotte Avenue, turning onto Mahoney then Main and heading north on Lake Shore Drive a little ways before they stopped. After setting the brake and looping the reins around a nearby post, he jumped down and gave her a hand to help her out of the carriage. It wasn't a long ride at all, and now they were just down the hill from the hotel. Why hadn't they just walked?

Alyssa wanted to ask Scott where they were headed, but he apparently had a certain place in mind. She was too tired to press, anyway. So, she let him lead. His gaze remained facing forward, and he carefully stepped through the sand, then around a few trees, until he finally stopped in between a pair of trees growing at odd angles.

He gently moved her to a specific spot, and she stood still as he positioned himself to face her.

"Alyssa Denham, you have turned my world upside down since the moment I first laid eyes on you. And I have only one question to ask." Scott reached into his coat pocket and pulled out a small blue box. He swept off his top hat, tucked it under his arm, set the box in his palm, and dropped to one knee, popping open the lid. "Is it you?"

Is it you? Alyssa drew her eyebrows together and stared down at Scott. It wasn't exactly the question she'd been expecting to come with such a beautiful ring. Where in the world had he—oh! The film! Her favorite film in the world. She looked around at their surroundings again. The trees, the sand, walking down by the lake, the hotel just up the hill, and now the line. She gasped. And the note he'd given her, too, the last time they'd seen each other. It all made sense.

"Is it?"

Scott's voice drew Alyssa's attention back to him. She bit her lower lip as her vision blurred. How could she reply with anything but the expected line? "Yes," she whispered with a wide smile.

An answering smile spread across his face. "Then, will you marry me?"

Scott scrambled to his feet in time to catch her as she threw herself into his arms. "I'll never make you ask twice," she replied.

He pulled away enough to remove the ring from the box and slide it onto the third finger of her left hand. She held out her hand and inspected the sparkling gem.

"It was my grandmother's," he said just before his mouth descended on hers, and she melded against him.

She'd avoided the truth for years, had let fear and pain keep her from realizing what her heart already knew. But today, she could say it with absolute certainty. She'd finally come home. Her grand adventure had just begun.

Group Discussion Guide

1. Discuss the five main characters in *A Grand Design*. Who, if any, did you find the most sympathetic? With which character did you relate best? Why?

2. In what way do the events of the novel affect each of the characters? How or to what degree does each of them change?

3. Have you ever been to Mackinac Island? If so, what did you like best about it? If not, have you ever been to a destination location? Where?

4. How is Alyssa introduced in this story? Did her experiences in the first chapter help you empathize with her, or did you roll your eyes and think that would never happen to one person all in one day?

5. What initial thoughts you did you have about the reason known only to Alyssa as to why she hadn't returned to Mackinac Island in fifteen years? Were you able to guess the reason or did you merely want to read on to find out the answer?

6. Alyssa arrived on the island carrying a load of past hurts. Yet she still managed to return. When was a time you were able to step past a prior hurt to engage and participate in something new?

7. According to this novel, what is it about the past that both draws us forward and leaves us stuck where we are? How can we be set free of the past? What are some methods you've used?

8. Compare and contrast Alyssa and Libby. How are they alike? How are they different? Now compare Scott and Ben. Do you currently or have you ever had a friend who is completely different from you? What about that friend keeps you loyal? Why do you stay friends?

9. Did the supporting characters add to or detract from the story? In what way? Who was your favorite supporting character and why?

10. What themes did you see in *A Grand Design*—either major or minor? How did those themes play out in the story?

11. How does the geography of a novel dictate its themes and characters? What role does setting play in *A Grand Design*? Could this story have taken place on any other island in the United States or even another country, or was Mackinac Island the necessary setting?

12. As Alyssa works her way through the various names on the list given to her by her grandmother, she starts piecing together not only the quilt her grandmother wanted finished but also bits of her grandmother's past. In what way does the quilt tie together the various stories of the characters?

13. Around three-fourths of the way through the book, Alyssa comes face to face with her past and the reason she hadn't returned to the island for so long. Put yourself in Alyssa's shoes, and then in Scott's. What would you have done in both instances?

14. What was your impression of Charlie Jarman? And how did you feel when he made a second appearance, albeit only through a reference and not his actual presence? Did you like the way that part of the story wrapped up? How would you have done it differently?

15. Certain people in Edith's past are welcoming to Alyssa and produce good memories. Others are quite the opposite. Is there a person, feeling, or event in your past that you'd want to revisit? Is there one you'd rather not revisit? Why?

16. Scott and Alyssa meet in Sadie's Ice Cream Parlor near the end of the book. Have you ever been in or do you know of a classic American ice cream parlor somewhere in the

U.S.? Where is it? What is your favorite ice cream flavor and why?

17. There are several movie tie-ins to the cult classic *Somewhere in Time*. Have you ever seen the movie? How well do you feel the homage paid in *A Grand Design* to this film was done? Would you have liked to have seen anything done differently?

18. Do you like it when books include bits of actual culture or reality, or do you prefer to merely have the setting described accurately, where the characters and experiences are completely fictional?

19. Reference was made about Scott's wealthy family, yet he kept it hidden from Alyssa when it might have become a topic of conversation, and it wasn't mentioned again. Do you feel this should have also had its loose ends tied, or did you not give it a second thought?

20. What other questions came to mind as you read this book? Were there any parts you felt didn't get covered or anything you wanted to see that wasn't included?

* Come find me on social media and share your answers to these questions. I love to hear from my readers. I'm also available via Skype or phone call if you make this book part of a book club reading. Please, get in touch.

We hope you enjoyed *A Grand Design* and that you will continue to read the Quilts of Love series of books from Abingdon Press. Here's an excerpt from *Hidden in the Stars* by Robin Caroll.

———✦———

1

Beep. Beep. Beep.

What on earth was beeping so loudly? And annoyingly.

Sophia Montgomery blinked. Brightness burst through the slit she'd managed to force open. She squeezed her eyes shut tight again and sucked in air.

A strange stench curled her nostrils. It was almost rancid . . . disinfectant mingled with sweat. That made no sense . . .

There had been two men, banging at the door. Barging in. Knives. Big knives. Grabbing her by the hair and throwing her to the floor. She hit her head against the leg of the chair. The coppery-metallic taste of blood filled her mouth.

Sophia tried again to open her eyes. W-what? she mouthed, but not a sound escaped. Burning shards closed around her throat as she tried to swallow against a gravelly resistance. Dear God, what's happening?

"Shh. Don't try to talk," a woman's crackly voice soothed. "The doctor will be here in a moment."

Doctor? Sophia struggled to sit, but every muscle in her body resisted, a sure sign she'd overdone at practice. Gentle hands eased her still. A cool, damp cloth stroked her forehead.

"You thought you could get away with it?" one of the men had yelled. His breath hissed against her face. Her neck.

She blinked again, this time prepared for the light. Or so she thought. The brilliance burned. She moaned and snapped her eyes closed.

"I'm sorry. Let me turn down the light," the woman whispered in her guttural toned voice.

Click. The sound echoed in Sophia's head.

"There. This should be better."

Sophia tried squinting a third time. While still brighter than the darkness she'd been comfortable in, the light wasn't so searing. She barely made out the figure of a woman at her side, hunching over her bed.

Wait a minute. Something wasn't right. Where was she? *God?*

"Well, good morning," a man's cheerful voice boomed.

Still squinting, Sophia shifted her gaze to the voice's origin. The fuzzy silhouette moved close to her.

"I'm Dr. Rhoads. Nod if you can hear me okay."

A doctor? What was going on? She nodded and forced her eyes open wider as pain ricocheted around her shoulders.

"Good." Cold hands touched her forehead. She must have reacted in some way because he chuckled softly and said, "Sorry. Everyone says I have the coldest hands in Arkansas."

Arkansas . . . but she lived in Texas. Plano. Close to the gym where she trained.

Training! *Lord, what is going on?*

The doctor shined a light in her eyes, searing them with its intensity. She snapped them closed and turned her head, moving out of his hold.

"I know it's uncomfortable, but I had to check your pupils."

Sophia forced her eyes open, willing them to focus on the man. She could now see his white coat. Dark hair. Big smile—too big.

She opened her mouth to ask what was going on, but razors sliced inside her throat.

"Don't try to talk. You sustained serious damage to your throat, including your vocal chords. We're treating the injury, and you've responded well, but you won't be able to talk until the swelling of your larynx subsides considerably."

She closed her eyes as scattered images raced through her mind. *Pinned to the floor. The bulky man straddling her, putting all his weight on her abdomen. His hands around her neck. Squeezing. Not enough oxygen! Can't breathe! Tighter. Tighter.*

She sucked in air and reached for her neck, but her arms wouldn't lift her hands. Red, hot arrows of pain shot from her shoulders down to her wrists. *Oh, God!* She opened her eyes wide and looked into her lap. Everything was in clear focus.

Sophia reclined in a hospital bed, the standard white sheet pulled up to her chest. Her arms sat on top of the sheet. Her hands were wrapped in gauze, big as footballs. Her right arm was in a cast up above her elbow.

The skinny man holding a knife to Mamochka's throat. Yelling. Demanding. The bulky one stepping on her right hand with his heavy, big boot. More pressure. The pain! Stop! Harder. Bones snapped. Please, please stop. The sobbing. Hers. Mamochka's.

The pounding of her heart echoed in her head, shoving aside the beeping sound getting faster and louder. *No, Lord. Please!*

"Calm down, Ms. Montgomery. Your blood pressure is too high. I don't want to have to give you anything right now," the doctor said.

"You must relax now, *MIlaya Moyna*," the older lady whispered as she patted Sophia's head with the cool cloth again. There was something so familiar about her . . . but . . . not.

"There you go," Dr. Rhoads said. "Breathe slowly. In through your nose and out through your mouth."

Even breathing hurt, but Sophia controlled her panic. Years of practicing self-control had made her a master despite her fears. Her hands. How would she compete?

"Well done, Ms. Montgomery. I'll go over your injuries with you in detail, if you're ready." Dr. Rhoads stared at her, a single brow raised.

She nodded, sending slicing pain shooting down her spine. Sophia set her jaw and refused to wince.

"Okay." The doctor reviewed her chart. "You have sustained a laryngeal fracture with some mucosal tearing. We're keeping you on voice rest to minimize edema, hematoma formation, and subcutaneous emphysema. We will continue the use of humidified air to reduce crust formation and transient ciliary dysfunction. We'll also continue treatment by use of systemic corticosteroids to retard inflammation, swelling, and fibrosis and to help prevent granulation tissue formation."

Tears threatened, but Sophia blinked them back and concentrated on what the doctor said.

"Since you sustained compound fractures of the larynx, we have you on systemic antibiotics to reduce the high risk of local infection and perichondritis, which may delay healing and promote airway stenosis. You're also taking antireflux medications to reduce granulation tissue formation and tracheal stenosis." Dr. Rhoads smiled. "Of course, this means you can't eat or drink anything for a few more days. Understand so far?"

Sophia swallowed instinctively and regretted it immediately. She didn't understand everything the good doctor said, but she got enough to know her throat was damaged enough that she couldn't talk or eat. Still, it didn't sound permanent, so it was something.

He leaned forward, letting his weight add strength to his hands closed around her throat. No! She couldn't see past his face anymore. His scowl. His eyes. They weren't filled with rage, but just . . . empty.

"Sophia? Do you understand?" Dr. Rhoads asked.

She ignored the scattered images and gave a little nod. Her head began to throb in cadence with her heartbeat.

"Good. Moving on . . . you've sustained serious, traumatic crush injuries to both of your hands. In surgery, we were able to remove all the tissue we couldn't salvage. We were able to repair most of the damaged blood vessels to reestablish circulation in your fingers. All the broken bones were realigned and stabilized with temporary pins called K-wires and screws. We repaired the damaged tendons and ligaments. Post-op, you're doing great. You should be able to begin physical therapy as soon as the bandages are off." Again, the doctor smiled.

"Tell us." He stepped down on her hand. Pain. Bones cracked. Sophia cried out. "Stop!" Mamochka screamed. "Tell us." He put all his weight on his foot. Bounced. Sophia screamed and tried to roll over to protect her hand. He slung her backward and plopped onto her hips, straddling her.

The image disappeared. She stared at her hands lying gauzed and lifeless in her lap. Everything within her wanted to scream . . . cry . . . hit something. Why was this doctor smiling? Didn't he get it? Her hands were her life! If she couldn't sustain her weight on her hands, her career was over. *Dear Lord, no. Anything but this.*

"О'кей *MIlaya Moyna*," the woman whispered.

No, it wasn't okay. And who was this woman to be calling Sophia *my sweet*? Especially in Russian.

Despite the excruciating pain the movement caused, she twisted her head to meet the woman's stare. Sophia was certain she'd never met the woman before, but there was something . . . her eyes. They were just like *Mamochka's.*

Could it be? The woman looked to be about the right age.

"Now," Dr. Rhoads interrupted her thoughts, "about your pelvic girdle fracture."

Her pelvis was busted, too? *He straddled her. Mamochka yelled out. Sophia kicked, trying to buck him off of her. She had to help her mother! He pinned her with his weight. Pain shot through her mid-section and hips as if she'd missed a dismount and fell off the balance beam. "You aren't going anywhere. Ever," he whispered as he leaned over her and wrapped his hands around her neck.*

Unaware of her agony, the doctor continued. "There's only one breaking point along the pelvic ring, with limited disruption to the pelvic bone and no internal or external bleeding. This means your pelvis is still secure despite the injury, and we can expect a prognosis of a quick, successful and complete recovery."

Great. So her pelvis would have a complete recovery. She could live without being able to talk. But would her hands totally recover? If so, when?

She closed her eyes, refusing the tears access. All her life, coaches and instructors had drilled into her head crying was not an option. Tears were to be saved for her pillow.

So many before her had sustained injuries and left the circuit, only to never return. Was it her fate? *Abba!*

"The rest of your injuries are minor cuts and bruises that should heal without incident. Several areas required stitches. You have a laceration at the back of your head where you were hit from behind—"

"Doctor," a man's deep voice cut off Dr. Rhoads.

Even though things were a little fuzzy to Sophia right now, even she didn't miss the frown etched into the doctor's brow.

Dr. Rhoads smiled at her. "Ms. Montgomery, you were very lucky. With the extent of your injuries, you could have been in a coma."

The other man cleared his throat.

The doctor frowned as he looked at her. "Now, if you feel up to it, there's a detective here who would like to ask you a few questions. Only if you feel up to it. Do you?"

A detective? She swallowed, then regretted it, but still nodded.

The doctor nodded and stepped back. "Keep it brief, please, Detective. She needs her rest." Dr. Rhoads patted the bed beside her feet. "I'll be back later to check on you."

"Ms. Montgomery, I'm Detective Frazier." There was the deep voice again, authoritative, but with a hint of danger.

Sophia stared at him as he stepped into her line of vision, and took a full inventory of her first impression of him. Hard to gauge his height since she was in the bed, but he stood taller than Dr. Rhoads. Even though it was short, his black hair held a wave. He had broad shoulders and muscular arms apparent under the short-sleeve, button-down Oxford shirt he wore. He was probably no more than twenty-eight or so, at least in her estimation based upon the weariness in his face covered in stubble. His chin was cut and his cheekbones well defined. His nose had been broken at least once. But it was his eyes drawing her attention. They were so dark they appeared like a bar of dark chocolate.

Then again, maybe it was just her distorted vision.

Detective Julian Frazier had been silently assessing Sophia Montgomery from the corner of her hospital room since she'd been brought here following her surgery. Over the last two and a half hours, he'd gotten over the shock of her appearance. He'd been a cop for enough years that the damage a victim sustained shouldn't have affected him, but he'd seen the pictures of Sophia Montgomery before the assault and to see her now . . .

He pushed off the wall he'd been leaning against and approached her bedside. "I have a few questions. Do you know who you are?"

She nodded, and unless he was imagining things, she actually rolled her eyes.

Attitude. Good. She'd need it. According to the doctors, she had a long, painful road to recovery in front of her. "Do you know where you are?"

She stared at him from her swollen, cut, and bruised face. There wasn't one square inch of her face and neck without some visible sign of her assault. Even her lips were cut and cracked as she tried to lick them. With her head resting on the pillow, she gave a nod.

"Do you know why you're here?" he asked, flexing and unflexing his fingers against the coolness of the hospital room. It might be June outside, but the nurses had set the thermostat low enough it felt like winter in the critical care ward.

She blinked.

Then again.

He met her stare with his own. Something about how small she was and the damage inflicted on her, yet she'd survived, nearly undid him. He'd overheard the nurses talking. They'd seen more people struck by vehicles with less damage than Sophia had endured. Whoever had attacked Sophia Montgomery and her mother had been especially vicious. Julian couldn't stand it. Whoever was responsible would face justice.

"Do you know why you're here?" he asked her again.

She tilted her head to the side. With her injuries, it had to hurt.

"You're unsure?"

She nodded.

Great. If she didn't remember anything, it would make his job so much more difficult. As it was, he was at a loss how he'd proceed at this point. With her extensive injuries, she couldn't speak and couldn't write, so how he was supposed to get her statement was more than a little confusing. He'd definitely have to think outside the box on this one.

She mouthed something. He couldn't tell what. She mouthed it again. It was one syllable, but he couldn't make it out. She mouthed it a third time.

"I'm sorry, but I don't understand." He snapped his fingers. "Let me get someone to help, okay?"

She nodded, but not before she shot him a look of pure frustration.

He could relate. Ever since he'd been called to the crime scene at almost eleven last night, frustration had been his constant companion. Frustrated this had happened. Frustrated no one had gotten there in time. Frustrated there were no immediate suspects.

Julian turned and stepped out of the hospital room, grabbing his cell phone from his hip. He quickly called his partner.

"She awake?" Brody Alexander asked without greeting. His partner was not one to waste time or breath with small talk when there was work to be done.

"Yep. Listen, we need to get Charlie up here ASAP to read her lips, so I can take her statement." Julian stared over his shoulder at Sophia's small and broken form lying so helplessly in the hospital bed. "And send some uniforms. I want someone posted by her room twenty-four-seven until we know what's going on."

"Got it." Brody hung up, business concluded. He might have an abrupt personality that had earned his reputation as an unappealing partner, but he suited Julian. After what happened with Eli, he wanted someone like Brody Alexander: all business.

He needed someone like Brody.

Julian put his cell back in its belt clip, strode back into the hospital room, and observed. It had taken the police some time to locate Alena Borin as Sophia's next of kin, only finding the connection through Sophia's mother's maiden name. The older woman fussed over Sophia, but Sophia didn't look like she recognized her grandmother. Maybe she had suffered some sort of brain injury in the attack. It would make his job much more difficult.

But not impossible. Because Julian refused to let whoever was behind this go unpunished. Someone would pay for this violence. He owed it to Sophia and her mother. The image of Sophia at the crime scene was one he would never forget. It would probably haunt him forever.

He returned to Sophia's bedside. Her eyes were guarded as she watched Alena Borin's every move: straightening the covers, gently bathing her forehead with the damp cloth. Sophia shifted her focus to collide with his gaze.

The uncertainty in her stare tugged at something buried deep within him. Something he didn't want to pull out and inspect. He cleared his throat until Ms. Borin gave him her attention.

"I've called in a lip reader to take Ms. Montgomery's statement," he said to her privately, in a low enough voice Sophia couldn't hear him. "This will take some time, and I'm sorry, but you can't be present. Why don't you go have some lunch?"

The older lady scowled at him, shaking her head.

"Ma'am, you don't have a choice. This is official police business."

She glanced down at Sophia, then back to him. "I will not leave her alone."

"She won't be alone. I'll be here the entire time, and there will be officers outside her door within the hour."

A long moment passed. She didn't say anything, nor did she move.

"Ma'am..."

Ms. Borin snatched up her purse. She smiled at Sophia. "I will be back in less than an hour, *MIlaya Moyna*." After patting the foot of the bed and throwing Julian another glare, she marched out of the hospital room.

Julian pulled the chair closer to the bed and sat. Sophia stared at him from behind her swollen face. He could read the wariness in her eyes as if it were a blazing neon sign.

"Do you know who that woman was?" He made a deliberate effort to speak just above a whisper level. The nurses had mentioned she'd probably have a horrible headache when she woke.

She shook her head—no, tilted it.

"You don't recognize her?"

She tilted her head again.

"You aren't sure who she is?"

A nod.

Julian stopped. Maybe he should wait for the lip reader, so he didn't misunderstand. She wasn't sure if she recognized and knew who Alena Borin was.

Sophia made a sound, but the pain it caused her marched across her face. She mouthed a single word, and this time, Julian understood exactly. "Who is she?" he asked.

She nodded.

He sat up straighter and looked her dead in the eye. "She's Alena Borin, your grandmother."

Want to learn more about author
Amber Stockton and check out other great
fiction from Abingdon Press?

Sign up for our fiction newsletter at
www.AbingdonPress.com
to read interviews with your favorite authors, find tips
for starting a reading group, and stay posted on what
new titles are on the horizon. It's a place to connect
with other fiction readers or post a
comment about this book.

Be sure to visit Amber online!

www.amberstockton.com
www.facebook.com/authoramberstockton
www.twitter.com/amberstockton

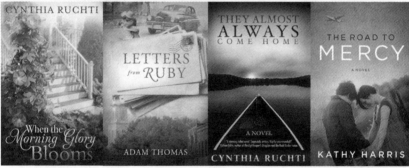